the RISE and FALL of MOUNT MAJESTIC

by Professor Barnabas Quill,
Historian of the Island at the Center
of Everything

Washed, dusted, translated, edited, and greatly
shortened for the rest of the world by

Jennifer Trafton

illustrated by

Brett Helquist

Dial Books for Young Readers
AN IMPRINT OF PENGUIN GROUP (USA) INC.

DIAL BOOKS FOR YOUNG READERS

A division of Penguin Young Readers Group
Published by The Penguin Group
Penguin Group (USA) Inc., 375 Hudson Street, New York, NY 10014, U.S.A.
Penguin Group (Canada), 90 Eglinton Avenue East, Suite 700, Toronto, Ontario,
Canada M4P 2Y3 (a division of Pearson Penguin Canada Inc.) • Penguin Books Ltd,
80 Strand, London WC2R 0RL, England • Penguin Ireland, 25 St. Stephen's Green,
Dublin 2, Ireland (a division of Penguin Books Ltd) • Penguin Group (Australia),
250 Camberwell Road, Camberwell, Victoria 3124, Australia (a division of Pearson
Australia Group Pty Ltd) • Penguin Books India Pvt Ltd, 11 Community Centre,
Panchsheel Park, New Delhi - 110 017, India • Penguin Group (NZ), 67 Apollo
Drive, Rosedale, North Shore 0632, New Zealand (a division of Pearson New
Zealand Ltd) • Penguin Books (South Africa) (Pty) Ltd, 24 Sturdee Avenue,
Rosebank, Johannesburg 2196, South Africa • Penguin Books Ltd, Registered
Offices: 80 Strand, London WC2R 0RL, England

Designed by Jennifer Kelly
Text set in Stempel Garamond

Printed in the U.S.A.

1 3 5 7 9 10 8 6 4 2

Library of Congress Cataloging-in-Publication Data
Trafton, Jennifer
The rise and fall of Mount Majestic / by Jennifer Trafton;
illustrated by Brett Helquist.   p. cm.
Summary: Ten-year-old Persimmony Smudge, who longs for heroic
adventures, overhears a secret that thrusts her into the middle of a
dangerous mission that could destroy the island on which she lives.
ISBN 978-0-8037-3375-6 (hardcover)
[1. Fairy tales. 2. Adventure and adventurers—Fiction.
3. Giants—Fiction.] I. Helquist, Brett, ill. II. Title.
PZ8.T71 Ri 2010
[Fic]—dc22   2009051659

For my parents

MAP of the ISLAND

Western
Shore

Boring villages
I've never
been to

Castl...

Mount
Majestic

Snoring Cave

Toddle

Feet of Swimming
Rumblebump

Bristlebend

Cow

Farmlands

Beyond

by Persimmony Smudge

Fishermen catching fish

Orchards

Tortoise

Leafeaters Secret door

City of Willowroot is underneath

Pepper Mill

Willow Woods

Candlenut

My Cottage

Theodore's Cottage

Restless mangrove with Worvil's house on top

Place where I buried dirty dishes

PROLOGUE

*T**here is a very* good possibility that you will not believe a word I say. Alas, it is the risk all historians take. The truest things are often the most unbelievable.

There is an island in the world, a small but lovely piece of earth, which its inhabitants call (rightly or wrongly) the Island at the Center of Everything. On the day before my story begins, it was as nearly perfect a place as an island in the world could reasonably expect to be.

The farmers whistled as they labored in their fields. The fishermen pulled in nets overflowing with fish. The Rumblebumps leaped from rock to rock along the Western Shore, splashing through tide pools and laughing at the wind. All over the island, people breathed the fresh, crisp breeze wafting in from the sea and let out long, lazy sighs of contentment.

And towering above them all was Mount Majestic, that beloved mound of grass and earth and stone. At the very top of the mountain stood the castle, and in a room somewhere the king sat cheerfully eating something.

Naturally there were troubles. Every so often some unfortunate soul wandered too far into the Willow Woods and was eaten by a tortoise. The people grumbled about the king; the king grumbled about the people; the Rumblebumps grumbled about no one and were ignored by everyone. The tired workers in the pepper mill trudged their weary circle. The Leafeaters collected their tears and waited anxiously for justice. The restless mangroves paced the forest floor searching for a spot to plant their roots and be content. And a young girl with mouse-colored hair and dirty feet hid under a threadbare quilt and dreamed of glory.

But despite some rumblings under the surface, the island drifted on the sea as peaceful and complacent as a cloud in a blue sky—until certain events changed it forever.

This is the story of those events.

I have thoroughly interviewed every eyewitness and triple-checked every detail. If the pages that follow are inspiring, enlightening, or life changing, I take full responsibility, but if there are any errors it is not my fault.

And so I invite you to take off your cloak of doubt, empty your pockets of all suspicions and jests, sit down before the roaring fire of my tale, and believe.

Chapter 1

In Which a Flying Hat Has Dire Consequences

On a dark night in a dense forest while the great wide wonder of the stormy sky threatened to burst through the trees and swallow her up, a girl lost her hat.

This would not be an event worth recording in the annals of history, except that the girl not only lost her hat, she lost her head. Which is to say, she panicked. When a gust of wind swept off her hat and sent it flying above the trees, she left the path she had been so carefully following to run after the vanishing blue speck. It is not surprising that when she finally recovered her head and sat down to think, she realized that she had now lost both her hat and her way home.

Out of the clumsiest moments of our lives, time can weave the most extraordinary tapestry of events. Who would have guessed that the fate of an entire kingdom depended upon a gust of wind, a flying hat, and a girl losing her way in a forest? Certainly she did not know what was to come, and on that night she imagined herself to be the most miserable person in the world.

The girl's name was Persimmony Smudge, which only added to her misery. She was ten years old, and ten whole years of living with that name was already too much. As far as she knew, only one person named *Smudge* had ever managed to be heroic, and he had disappeared.

Persimmony angrily kicked a stone (which, unfortunately for her toe, remained in place). "It's all Prunella's fault!" she cried. "If she hadn't pestered me about sweeping the floor right in the middle of my glorious dream about rescuing a baby from the teeth of a murderous alligator, I would never have thrown the broom across the room. Then the broom would never have hit the Giving Pot, and I wouldn't be here trudging through the Willow Woods in the middle of the night to fetch a new pot from Theodore. And with a storm coming too!"

She shivered, not so much from the cold as from

the thought of her mother returning home in the morning to find the Giving Pot and the new hat gone (not to mention her daughter). She could just imagine her punishments. No more trips into town. No more afternoons sneaking out to the seashore. Nothing but chores. She would end her life as a shriveled old woman surrounded by brooms and darning needles and mixing spoons and rags. Doomed—all because of her sister—to an everlasting existence of sweeping and dusting and stirring and mending. She could hardly bear the thought.

That's why she had run straight for the path to Theodore's cottage in the first place. If it was a choice between braving the woods at night or braving her mother's anger, well, she would take her chances with the woods. *Braving the woods at night to save the family from a slow, agonizing death by starvation* did have such a heroic sound to it. Well, maybe they wouldn't exactly die of *starvation* without the Giving Pot, but they would certainly be very hungry.

But then her hat had blown away, and with it all of her heroism. It was a large-brimmed blue hat with embroidered fruit all over it. It looked more like a drowning apple tree than a hat, but she loved it. Usually she felt invisible—a poor girl with worn-out clothes, a forgettable face, and hair that was neither golden yellow nor chocolate brown nor fiery red, but rather like dirty dishwater. People didn't notice her, but they noticed her hat. It made her feel less Smudge-like.

All at once, the sky burst through. White streaks of lightning lit up the blackness that had gathered over the trees. Thunder made the ground tremble. A sudden downpour drenched the Willow Woods.

Persimmony jumped to her feet, holding her arms helplessly over her head. She was angry, and afraid, and hungry, and wet. So she did the only thing she could do: She started to dance. She leaped and spun and flung out her arms. Her bare feet skipped and slid and squished in the mud. *Take that, you thunder!* She kicked her heels high. *Take that, you storm!* She twirled in circles until she was dizzy and out of breath and her fear had turned into laughing.

Then she took one last leap into the wet branches of the nearest willow. She clasped her arms around them and swung upward into the night sky. When she swung back, she bumped into the tree trunk, slid down into the dark, dry space around it, and lay there on the ground, panting.

As Persimmony would have remembered if she

had been thinking clearly, disturbing a willow tree at night is even more foolish than leaving a path to run after a flying hat. High above in the willow's canopy of leaves, two round, yellow eyes slowly appeared. A black shape began to creep noiselessly down the trunk. There was a flash of lightning that made the woods suddenly as bright as day, and in that moment Persimmony saw the tortoise.

There had been a time, when she was very, very young and only acquainted with the lumbering, clumsy sea turtles that played with her by the shore, when Persimmony had laughed at the idea of being frightened by a tortoise. *A poison-tongued jumping tortoise?* Faster than a human? Living in a willow tree? She had thought it was another of her mother's tricks to keep her out of the woods and at home. Then she had learned better.

There is absolutely nothing laughable about a poison-tongued jumping tortoise when you are standing two feet away from it.

Crouched at the base of the trunk, it was nearly as tall as she was. Its domed shell of black, bony plates was rimmed with sharp spikes, and its legs were several times the size of its head. The tortoise's eyes were fixed steadily on her, and from underneath its pointed snout slid a long, snakelike tongue—a tongue

so poisonous that a single lick would put a swift end to her. Persimmony saw all of this in a few seconds, and then the night was black again.

This was not how it was supposed to happen. She had told the story to herself hundreds of times, lying in her bed with the quilt pulled over her head and imagining that she was the last remaining defender of the town of Candlenut as it was being ravaged by a pack of poison-tongued tortoises. The townspeople—and her mother and sister—and in some versions the king and his entire court—cowered in the background weeping and crying out, "Persimmony, you are our only hope! Forgive us for thinking you were nothing but a basket maker's daughter, a nobody, a Smudge! Forgive us for ignoring you! Save us, Persimmony, save us!" And then she would smile sweetly and walk up to the leader of the tortoises and plunge a knife into—

But now she was alone, without an admiring audience or victims to be rescued, without a knife or a slingshot or anything at all to defend herself. Now the woods were dark and the rain was pelting the ground like hail and she was hopelessly lost, and even if she was to put up a valiant fight before she died, no one would ever know and she would never get a new pot from Theodore or make it home to tell her mother that it was all Prunella's fault.

"DON'T YOU DARE EAT ME AFTER ALL I'VE BEEN THROUGH TODAY!" she yelled.

The tortoise responded with a hiss as piercing as a scream.

Persimmony decided that it was safer to run than to scream back, so she ran through the freezing rain and the darkness, over and under and around what she could not see—except in moments, when the lightning lit up the world like a huge candle only to be blown out again by the wind.

The ground trembled under the weight of the tortoise as it jumped after her, plowing through the trees in its way. BUMP! THUD! CRASH!

At last Persimmony spied a large fallen tree trunk, and she sprinted over it and ducked in its shadow, pressing against the soft layer of moss that covered it. To her surprise, the moss gave way behind her. She tumbled backward and suddenly found herself *inside* the tree. The trunk was hollow, like a tunnel, and the moss had been covering a small hole in the side. What a perfect hiding place! If only the tortoise had not seen her! But it had. Its shell scraped against the bark as it scrambled over the tree trunk. Persimmony squeezed farther back into the dark tunnel—just as the tortoise thrust its head straight into the hole and began to come in after her.

It was lucky for Persimmony that the shell of the poison-tongued jumping tortoise was so much larger than its brain, and also larger than the hole in the tree trunk. Just as the snapping jaws and outstretched tongue had almost reached her face, the tortoise's shell got stuck and wouldn't move forward another inch. Hissing in fury, the tortoise kicked and rolled and stretched its neck as far as it could, but Persimmony was beyond its reach. It finally withdrew in disappointment.

But it did not leave. Instead, it sat down right outside the hole, blocking Persimmony's exit.

"Oh, I should never have gotten out of bed this morning!" said Persimmony, forgetting that to be alive and uneaten was a miracle worthy of notice. She waited and waited in the pitch-black tunnel, until the sound of the pouring rain was drowned out by the harsh rattle of the tortoise's snoring. At last, she lay down inside the cramped space and fell asleep, too tired even to pout over her misfortune. Too tired, in fact, to hear the faint shudder of a sigh behind her in the dark recesses of the tree trunk.

A broom. A hat. A girl. A hole.

Such small things in a big world. But without the small things, there would be no story to tell, and—most importantly—I would not still be alive to tell it.

Chapter 2

In Which Tragedy Besets the Royal House

On the very evening that Persimmony Smudge lost her hat in the middle of the Willow Woods, young King Lucas the Loftier ran out of pepper in the middle of his supper.

He had already eaten three lobsters, four bowls of shrimp, eleven crab cakes, two pumpkin pies, and a platter full of pineapple chunks swimming in coconut sauce. He was just about to start on his favorite dish, the crowning glory of his evening meal: sweet potato soup.

The king's life had many delights—wealth, power, comfortable mattresses, subjects bowing at his feet and wishing he would live forever, servants scratching that part of his back that he could never quite reach—but what delighted King Lucas above all things (except one) was sweet potato soup. That one thing he loved most, the highest delight of his life, was pepper. So when the large, steaming hot bowl of soup appeared on the table, he immediately reached for the pepper shaker and turned it upside down.

Nothing happened.

He shook it. He smacked it. He sat on it. He stood on the table and jumped up and down with the pepper shaker until his face had turned as red as

the lobsters and his soup had splashed all over the floor. But still nothing came out.

"Nubbins! Nubbins! You stupid oaf, get in here!"

A terrified steward peeked through the doorway. Though he was five times the age of the king and twice his height, the aging servant bowed with the nervousness of a child about to be punished. "Yes?" he squeaked. "Is there something wrong with Your Highness's dinner?"

"This pepper shaker is broken!" yelled Lucas, thrusting it into the steward's trembling hands. "Nothing comes out! FIX IT!" His crown slid down on his forehead and he shoved it back furiously.

The poor steward answered, "Right. Of course. Pepper shakers can be tricky little things. They have minds of their own, you know. Have you tried salt, Your Highness? Salt can be much more cooperative. Or ginger, perhaps?"

"No!" said Lucas.

"Cinnamon?"

"I want pepper."

"Right, right. Pepper. Well, the thing is, Your Highness, the thing—is—that—ha-ha! Well, you DO go through a lot of pepper in a day. Not that I blame you, of course! Pepper is, after all, one of the greatest delights in life. It just isn't—um—one of the most—"

"What? One of the most what?"

"Abundant, Your Highness."

"Will you stop blabbering and tell me why my pepper shaker won't work?"

"Because there's no more pepper."

"*What?*"

"The pepper storeroom is clean empty, and I'm afraid it may be several weeks before we get a new supply from the pepper mill."

"Then they'll just have to work harder. I need more pepper. I can't live without pepper! Don't you know that my thirteenth birthday is less than two weeks away? How can I have a birthday party without any pepper to serve my guests? It would be . . . It would be . . . It would be extremely discumbersome-bubblating."

"I beg your pardon, Your Highness, but I believe you mean discombobulating."

"How *dare* you tell me what I mean, Nubbins?"

"Of course, of course, forgive me! I did not hear you correctly at first. I often feel discumbersome-bubblated myself."

"You do not. No one can feel discumbersomebub-blated except a king."

"Your Highness," the steward tried again, anxiously tying the thumbs of his gloves together, "the pepper mill workers are already working twenty hours a day. They barely have enough time to sleep, or eat, or see their families. Mr. Fulcrumb says he can get no more work out of them. Perhaps, Your Highness, if you go down there and see for yourself—"

"Of course I won't go down! Mr. Fulcrumb will just have to find more workers," said Lucas. "Tell him to go out and capture a few dozen people to work in the mill, and if they refuse, they will be arrested for treason. If I don't have a full pepper shaker soon, *somebody is going to regret it.*"

The steward mumbled a promise and disappeared.

King Lucas sank back in his chair and pushed his crown out of his eyes. "Oh, I am the most miserable person in the world!" he cried. He was in such low spirits that the only thing to do was to put on his best robe (the one embroidered with palm trees and studded with pearls where the coconuts should be), go to the very top of the highest tower in the castle, and look out over his kingdom.

There were four windows at the top of this tower. By moving from one window to the other, King Lucas could see the entire island sloping down from Mount Majestic toward the sea. To the north, the orchards were ripe with bananas, oranges, mangoes, and papayas for his breakfast, and the fishermen's boats drifted in the bay gathering tuna for his lunch. To the south, the fields teemed with vegetables and spices, and the villagers toiled to send him their finest wares. To the east, the forest lay like a thick green blanket, full of the loveliest wood for furniture and hand-carved frames for all of his portraits. To the west, goats grazed upon the grassy hills above the great stone cliffs where the waves sent thundering applause up to his listening ears.

But tonight all of that beauty was overshadowed by darkness and battered by wind and rain.

No more pepper! Why, it was worse than the most painful toothache. Worse than waking up to find a cockroach on your pillow. Worse than going swimming and being attacked by a stinging jellyfish and then dying very, very slowly. There was nothing in the world so terrible as expecting sweet potato soup with pepper and being left with only soup.

Go down there and see for yourself? What an idea! He may as well strip naked and run into a field of mad cattle. No, it was being lofty that made a king a king. *Down there* he would just be a boy wearing a crown that was too big for him.

Perhaps he was getting soft. Perhaps his people did not respect him enough. Very well, then, he would insist on having *two* pepper shakers at every meal. If the shoemaker brought him three pairs of boots, he would demand six. If a woodsman chopped down a tree, he would demand a forest.

The thought of trees made him remember an annoying little event that had happened during supper the week before. A parchment had arrived at the castle strapped to the back of a large gopher, and this is what was written:

To His Majesty King Lucas the Loftier, revered monarch over the Island at the Center of Everything and all the creatures that live within its shores:

Long live the king, and may his towers never fall.

We, the Leafeaters of Willowroot, humbly bring before the king's eyes this list of grievances:

Firstly and most reprehensibly, that you have been secretly cutting down trees in the Willow Woods, though you know full well that we depend on the leaves of these trees for our sustenance, livelihood, continuation, and indeed our very dinners.

Secondly, that you have stolen our trees for the purpose of making chairs and tables and beds and clocks and picture frames to beautify your own castle, when you already had enough chairs and tables and beds and clocks and picture frames to satisfy a hundred kings, and then some.

Thirdly, that you did not say "please" before you did it, nor did you say "thank you" afterward.

Fourthly, that according to trustworthy reports you repeatedly use incorrect grammar, lick your plate at meals, interrupt others while they speak, and scorn centuries of hallowed tradition, and therefore you stand against everything that the Leafeater people hold most dear.

For these reasons, it is with great sorrow that the Leafeaters, formerly your loyal subjects, must hereby demand an apology, the replanting of our lost trees, and an immediate stop to all such disgusting behaviors . . . or else.

Yours respectfully,
Rhule Rhodshod, the Chief of the Leafeaters

How dare those tunnel-dwelling, cowardly, pompous sticks-in-the-mud tell him what to do and what not to do with his own trees?

He had written a swift reply:

To Rhule Rhodshod, the stuffed-shirt, leaf-eating idiot who calls himself a chief:

Oh, shut up.

Yours disdainfully,
   King Lucas the Loftier
   (that is, loftier than YOU)

Well, he reflected now, at least in *that* circumstance he had acted in a proper kingly manner. He felt better. There at the tip-top of the castle, in the center of a storm, with nothing above him but the moon and the stars half hidden by black clouds, King Lucas basked in the knowledge that he was loftier than everything else that existed. Then he felt more than ever like "His Royal *High*-ness."

Of course, in order to be *truly* highest, he had to stand at the top of the tower at noon, when the peak of Mount Majestic reached its highest point. In the morning, the mountain was still swelling and rising, and after noon it sank slowly until midnight, when it would begin to rise again—and so on and so forth, rising and falling like a wave on the sea, every day since the beginning of time (or at least for as long as anyone could remember). When it was at its lowest point, the mountain was like a huge hill stretching across the island from the western cliffs to the Willow Woods. And when it was at its pinnacle, it was truly majestic indeed.

To be sure, there were minor inconveniences to living on top of a moving mountain. The furniture had to be nailed to the floor and the china wrapped in cotton in the cupboards. Sometimes a sudden shift of the earth under the king's feet sent him careening into his scullery maid's arms, which was quite embarrassing, and sometimes his bowl of soup slid down to the opposite end of the table just as he was about to dip his spoon into it. And those who lived at the mountain's foot had to build very strong roofs on their houses to protect against rockslides. Apart from these occasional mishaps, however, nobody bothered much about the mountain's behavior. It had always been like this, and it always would be.

Or so they believed.

⊂⊚ Chapter 3 ⊚⊃

In Which Persimmony Hears Something She Shouldn't

It was very late before the thunder faded to a distant grumbling. Long before the sun rose, Persimmony was nudged awake by a different sound.

"Prunella, I'm trying to sleep," she mumbled. Then the dampness of her dress and the discomfort of her position reminded her of where she was, and she realized that the voice she heard speaking did not belong to her sister.

"There is nothing like the taste of green maple leaf stew," the voice said, "when the leaves have been threshed by the wind and seasoned by spring rain."

"True," said a second voice, "though I've always considered roasted pine needles to be a delicacy beyond compare. I ate nearly a whole wheelbarrow full of them after the last Ceremony of Tears . . . Here, do you need another sack? Yours is almost full."

The voices were only a few feet away, just beside the tree trunk in which Persimmony lay hidden. *Leafeaters.* Her mind was numb with sleepiness, but she was awake enough to feel a shiver of nervousness. Leafeaters posed no danger when she passed them in broad daylight in the Candlenut market, but if they found her alone at night in the woods—*their* woods—there was no telling what could happen.

"Pardon me, distinguished beast, but will you kindly move aside to make room for an old friend with an aching back?" the first voice said more loudly. Then, with a polite snort (I've been assured there is such a thing, though I've never been privileged to hear it), the poison-tongued jumping tortoise plodded off into the forest. Two legs appeared right in front of Persimmony's eyes—thin, sticklike legs, barely visible in the dim moonlight—and the trunk rocked slightly as someone sat down on top of it. "We'll have to gather as many leaves as we can," he continued. "There is no telling how long we'll even have a forest, if the king keeps cutting down trees. That letter he wrote to our chief!

Why, it's an offense beyond all offenses the Leafeaters have suffered, and we have suffered many at the hands of those Sunspitters."

"There is nothing to worry about," said the second voice. "He will get his comeuppance soon enough when we reach the center of the mountain. He was foolish if he thought he could keep the gold buried underneath the castle a secret!"

"Yes, it's disgraceful how Sunspitters never believe the prophecies of the Lyre-That-Never-Lies until it tells them something they want to hear," said the first voice. "Well, we'll beat him to his treasure and not give him any of it until he grants us what we ask. He's more than a fool—he is a villain and he deserves to be whipped, scolded, hanged until he is thoroughly dead, and then sent to bed without supper."

"Now, now, remember rule number seventeen of the Code of Courtesy: 'It is unkind to kill anything unless it is about to eat you. And if you are forced to kill any living thing, make sure you bow first.'"

"I beg your pardon. Are you lecturing me? You're barely a green bud on the family tree, Rheuben. When you have been alive as long as I have, you'll realize that those *aboveground* have no sense of decency, no appreciation for beauty, and above all *no manners*. Give me ten years in a room with one of them, and

I assure you I wouldn't be able to teach him to say *please* to a beetle!"

"I meant no disrespect, sir. I admit they do show an appalling disregard for proper speech. But there are many beautiful things aboveground. Once I saw a farmer pause in his field, gaze up at the purple sunset, and smile. Surely that shows a taste for loveliness?"

"*Smile*? Beauty is a serious thing—utterly serious! That farmer was probably thinking of his supper."

"I'm sure these things are far above my understanding," the second voice said soothingly.

"Very well, you're forgiven. Oh, my creaking knee! I'll not be much use for leaf gathering if my rheumatism gets any worse. At least I've not been asked to help with the digging. How far have they progressed?"

"The outskirts of Willowroot already lie under the westernmost edge of the woods. Chief Rhule says they will most likely penetrate the foot of the mountain in a matter of days. I only wish I could paint as fast as they can dig. My brushes are completely worn out, and I'll need to go up to Candlenut to buy more very soon."

"Oh bother, I shall have to accompany you. I need more pepper. The diggers are working so hard that my cooks and I are barely making enough stew to feed them. These leaves we've gathered tonight will get us through another day, at least."

"Well, I have all I can carry for now. Shall we return?"

The legs stirred and the tree trunk rocked again as the old Leafeater rose to his feet. "You first."

"No, no, I insist: You first."

"I wouldn't dream of it. You go first."

"Unthinkable! I will not go before you."

"Oh, well, really, if it will make you happy."

"Yes . . . please."

The voices died away quickly—as though the owners had suddenly passed through a doorway rather than simply walked off into the woods. Something tugged at Persimmony's mind—something important they had said—but she couldn't remember what.

She thought, *The tortoise is gone. I should go home.*

She thought, *I don't think roasted pine needles would taste good at all.*

And then she fell back asleep.

Chapter 4

IN WHICH HOME IS WHERE THE HEARTACHE IS

The storm clouds passed. The dawn broke. The sun rose, and so did the mountain.

At the edge of the Willow Woods, a broom flew through the window of a cottage and landed in a mud puddle.

"Oh, Mother, it wasn't my fault!" wailed a girl who was normally quite pretty but whose face was now swollen with crying and buried in her apron. "I tried to do as you said, I really did. I dusted and washed and sorted and folded and mended. But Persimmony was daydreaming as usual and I only asked her to sweep the floor and then she threw the broom across the room and it broke the Giving Pot and by the time I had finished picking up all the little pieces

she was gone. But I did find the sewing needle you lost three months ago."

"Prunella, my foolish child, my delight, my darling, my dolt of a daughter! I'd rather you had lost the sewing needle and found your sister!"

Prunella broke down in another fit of crying. She had tried so hard. She really had. The teacups were so neatly stacked.

Mrs. Smudge's eyes were sharp, and her hair was swept back tightly in a bun and tied with a handkerchief that was an odd mixture of faded purple and yellow stripes. It had not taken her long to search the cottage for her missing child, since the room only contained three small, lumpy beds, a table with a broken leg, a wooden washbasin filled with newly cleaned dishes, and a huge fireplace with a pot for cooking. The rest of the space was taken up with piles of branches and vines waiting to be woven into baskets. Of course, there was also the hole in the corner and the ladder leading to the cellar underground—but Persimmony never went down there. It was too small to imagine in, she always said.

There were no books in the cottage because Persimmony's mother had a moral objection to education. She also had a moral objection to shoes, barbershops, dancing, oysters, and freckles, among other things. Since Persimmony insisted on playing outdoors and her fair skin was prone to freckles, Mrs. Smudge had finally overcome her moral objection to hats and bought one a week ago. It was the only one she could afford because it was a ridiculous thing and the shopkeeper was anxious to get rid of it.

"So she took the hat, did she?" said Mrs. Smudge, seeing the bare hook on the wall. "Does she think I am made of money, that I can buy a new hat every time she decides to run off with one? Oh, the poor thing! What has become of her? She could have been eaten by a tortoise, or trampled by a restless mangrove, or kidnapped by the Leafeaters and dragged underground never to be seen again! At the very least she is soaking wet. Serves her right, the disobedient imp. Throw a broom and break my Giving Pot! She probably went to fetch a new one from old Theodore, hoping I wouldn't notice. Oh, she is too much like her father, *too* much—always brave and never sensible! Well, she can't have gotten far. Come, Prunella, we'll find her before dinnertime, I'm sure. An acorn never falls far from the tree, and a hungry stomach never wanders far from the kitchen, that's what I always say. But oh, my poor little lost lamb, my thoughtless, spoiled hooligan!"

"But Mother, why are we going to look for acorns?"

Prunella said, blowing her nose in her apron. "Are we going to eat them for dinner now that the Giving Pot won't give us any more bread?"

"We're not looking for acorns," Mrs. Smudge said impatiently, "we are looking for your sister."

"But you just said—"

"*Prunella Smudge!*"

"Yes, Mother."

Persimmony's mother and sister could have searched until many dinners had passed without ever finding Persimmony, who had awakened to a cold, clammy bed, a centipede crawling up her arm, and a cramp in her leg—not exactly the way to start off the morning on the right foot.

The first thing she did was stretch out her cramped leg as far as she could into the hollow tree trunk. Her foot met something soft, and there was a muffled yelp.

Persimmony bolted out of the hole into the sunshine. "Who's there?" she exclaimed, backing away from the tree trunk.

From the darkness of the hole came a hesitant reply: "W-W-W-Worvil."

Persimmony crept closer, straining to see the hidden speaker while still keeping a safe distance from the tree. She picked up a large stick. "Who are you?" she said. "Have you—have you been there all night?" A very unpleasant sensation traveled down her spine. "Come out so I can see you!"

There was a long pause, then out of the hollow tree trunk came a pink, bald head with a deeply lined brow. Out came shoulders as stooped as if they bore the weight of an entire mountain. Out came a short body nearly swimming in clothes several sizes too big for it, with sleeves and trouser legs rolled up thickly and covered with mud and beetles. The wide, round, red-rimmed eyes that stared up into Persimmony's were the eyes of someone who may have been happy once or twice in his life, but far too long ago to remember now. Though he was obviously not a child, he only came up to her shoulders—as if someone had taken a grown-up man and squashed him. He reminded her of a potato: small and lumpy and utterly unadventurous.

"Put the stick down! Oh please, put the stick down!" the little man cried. "Don't you know you could *hurt* someone?"

Persimmony decided she had nothing to fear from a person obviously terrified of her, so she put the stick down and sat on a rock with a sigh of relief. "I'm Persimmony," she said, "and I have had the worst night in history. You'll never believe what I've been through. My hat flew away, and I got drenched in a thunderstorm, and a poison-tongued jumping tortoise chased me through the woods and nearly killed me, and I've had nothing to eat since lunch yesterday, and I'm so hungry I could eat a—a—well, something very, very big. As long as it doesn't taste like my mother's cooking."

Worvil gazed at her with bottomless sympathy.

"And the worst part of all," she continued miserably, "is that I'm lost and I have no idea how to get home again."

"Oh, I can fix that." Worvil brightened a bit. "I was so afraid I'd get lost in the woods that I made a map. It's in my house."

"How far away is your house?"

"Right beyond those trees over there. In a clearing." Worvil pointed, and the two began picking their way through the thick shrubbery toward the spot.

"If your house is nearby, why did you spend the night in the tree trunk?"

"I was on my way home, but *it* came after me before I could get there."

"The poison-tongued jumping tortoise?"

"No, the cricket. And then the rain came, and then you came, and then the Leafeaters—" He broke off.

"The *what*?" A sudden memory washed over

her—voices in the night, spindly legs, a letter from the king, gold under the mountain, digging. "So you heard them too! It wasn't a dream!"

"No, no, I didn't hear a word. Not about kings or gold or anything. I was asleep. Here's the clearing up ahead. My house is—" Worvil stopped so suddenly that Persimmony bumped into him. There was certainly a clearing, and a lot of churned-up earth in the center of it, but no house in sight.

Worvil fell on his knees and gripped his bald head in his stubby hands. "Not again!" he cried. "I knew it! I *am* the most miserable person in the whole world!"

Persimmony was just about to say that if you're silly enough to lose your own house, you're better off keeping your map in your pocket, but Worvil was already dashing into the woods again.

"Hey!" yelled Persimmony, following him. "Where are you going? Stop! Wait for me!"

But Worvil didn't slow down, and he ran remarkably fast for someone with such short legs and such long trousers. "It all started on my sixth birthday," he wailed as he ran. "The whole family was gathered, and I knocked over the cake with all its candles and burned the house down. I alone survived."

"That's terrible," said Persimmony breathlessly, truly feeling sorry for him but wondering what this had to do with finding his house in the woods.

"That's when I lost all my hair—it burned off and never grew back. After that I moved in with my uncle on the northern coast. My uncle was a fisherman, you see, and taught me how to fish. But one day I was out fishing and he was in the cottage taking a nap, and a huge wave swept the cottage out to sea with my uncle inside."

"I really am sorry, but don't you think we should be marking our trail or something?"

"Then I moved south and tried my hand at being a farmer," he continued, panting and wheezing as Persimmony struggled to keep up. "That was the year of the Great Sweet Potato Famine when the crops rebelled and refused to produce anything but turnips, and of course, no one wanted to eat turnips. And so my farm failed, and I had to move to Candlenut to be apprenticed to a beekeeper whose hives were just downwind of the pepper mill. But I'm allergic to pepper, you see, and one time I sneezed so hard that I cracked a rib, which was bad enough, but the sneeze disturbed the bees so much that they stung me thirteen times, and I discovered that I'm also allergic to bee stings. And I almost died. So of course I had to move again."

Persimmony had a strong feeling that she should

have paid more attention to the place they had come from and the direction they had taken. But the fear of being abandoned by Worvil in an unfamiliar part of the woods drove her on.

"So I moved out to the middle of a field," he was saying, "with no candles, no sea, no crops, no pepper mills, no bees, and no roof above me, and I lived on nuts and berries and took baths in the rain and dried off in the sun, and I was almost content—until one day an eagle flying overhead mistook my bald head for a rock and dropped a turtle on it, and I almost died again. I've never been able to add or subtract right since. So I moved to the Willow Woods and built a house in the low branches of a mangrove tree. How was I supposed to know it was a *restless* mangrove?" He spotted something over to the right and ran with more determination than ever. "Wait!" he cried. "Come back with my house!"

Just then, Persimmony saw what they were chasing.

It was indeed a mangrove tree—a small one—walking on the tips of its sprawling, tangled web of roots. The dwelling in its upper branches looked less like a house and more like a badly made nest of wooden boards, sticks, and dried mud with a patched-together tent for a roof. A sign was nailed to the side of the trunk:

NO ONE LIVES HERE.
PLEASE GO AWAY.

Standing still, the roots would have made a perfect ladder by which one could climb to the house above. But moving, they were like the legs of a giant spider crawling across the forest floor. The tree was evidently out for a leisurely morning stroll, but as Worvil got closer it started walking faster. The house at its top shook and rattled. Chunks of the walls started falling to the ground.

With a look of utter desperation, like a man whose last hope in the world is running the opposite direction, Worvil flung himself onto the nearest root. He bounced up and down, holding on to the root and shouting, "Oh, please, please, stop . . . Have pity on me . . . What have I ever done to you?"

Persimmony gasped and called out, "Hold on! I'll save you!" though she had no idea how. She leaped forward and grabbed Worvil's leg, but that only unrolled his trousers, and she ended up with her fists full of trouser cuffs, bumping and rolling in the dirt after the fleeing tree. "LET GO!" she cried, and choked on a tuft of grass. But then the tree raised the root high and gave a *kick*, and both Worvil and Persimmony sailed through the air and landed in a pile of wet leaves. The mangrove disappeared into the forest.

Persimmony rolled off Worvil's stomach and sat up. "Are you all right?" she asked.

Worvil lay flat on his back staring forlornly at the sky. "The last three times this happened," he said, "I was inside the house. Once a pot fell on my head and knocked me unconscious, but at least I still woke up in my own home (even if it was on the other side of the woods). That's why I started making a map."

"Why don't you just build another house in a tree that stays put?"

"You mean move *again*?" he groaned.

"Well, anyway, that was brave of you, jumping onto a moving tree like that," she said, trying to make him feel better.

Worvil sat up quickly. "Brave? Was that *brave*? Oh, no! I'll never do it again, I promise."

"But someday you might—"

"DON'T! Don't say that word!"

"What word? I didn't even get a chance to finish!"

"You said *might!*" Worvil covered his face with his hands. "Of all the words that have ever been invented, that is the worst. All of the terror in the world hangs on the word *might*. The Leafeaters *might* kidnap me and keep me locked up underground forever. They *might* tie me to a tree and leave me to be eaten by poison-tongued jumping tortoises. A hurricane *might* flood the Willow Woods and both of us drown . . ."

"Well, there certainly isn't much chance of that happening!" said Persimmony. "The sun is shining and there isn't a cloud in the sky."

"But it *might*. Anything *might* happen."

"Right. You *might* find your house again and live happily ever after."

"But I might *not*."

Persimmony stared at Worvil and discovered that she liked him. He was a coward, certainly, but he had Imagination. She like people with Imagination.

Something was still tugging at her mind. "Do you believe the Leafeaters really kidnap people and lock them up underground?"

Worvil carefully rolled up the trouser leg that Persimmony had unrolled when she grabbed him. "I don't know if they *do*, but they *might*. Why else would they build a secret city underground, if not to hide people that they don't like?"

"It's just that—it's just that I have a father, or I had a father—"

"I'm sorry," said Worvil.

"Why?"

"That you *had* him, but you don't *have* him. Did he die a terrible, miserable death?"

"NO! Well, at least, I don't think so. How can you die a terrible, miserable death on an island and no one know about it?"

"Then you still *have* a father?"

"No—I mean yes—except that I don't *have* him. I mean I don't know where he is. He disappeared when I was very little, and I don't remember him at all."

"I remember my father," sighed Worvil. "Sometimes remembering isn't all it's cracked up to be."

"*My* father is a hero," Persimmony said proudly. "I know because Mother always said that he was the bravest man she had ever met and that she wished he had been cowardly and stayed home instead. I think that means he disappeared doing something very brave, don't you? She won't tell me."

In fact, no amount of questions could drag out of her mother much more than "Your father is a *father*, that's what he is!" or "Handsome is as handsome does, oh! and he did it so handsomely too. Go wash your hands for supper." She wouldn't say whether or not he whistled, or whether his ears got taller when he smiled, or what color his eyes were in the dark, or what happened when he disappeared. Persimmony had once asked Prunella, who was two years older, whether she remembered anything at all, and Prunella had just stared out the window for a moment and said, "He made little animals out of twigs and pine needles. He made me a turtle once. I don't know where it went." And then, rubbing away tears with her apron and tucking her feet underneath her skirt, she had gone back to knitting a stocking.

Prunella was so *dull*. Didn't she understand that when you were the daughter of a hero, especially a mysteriously disappeared hero, you *couldn't* just sit around knitting stockings all day? You were meant to do important things, like cure a horrible disease, or discover a new color, or tame wild donkeys, or teach mosquitoes to ask nicely before biting.

For a long time, Persimmony had imagined that her father was on a secret mission for the king, living in disguise while he battled treacherous enemies— until recently when she told Theodore of her idea, and Theodore informed her that the king was only twelve years old. This had shocked her, for she thought that all kings were born very old and very wise, with silver beards on their noble, wrinkled faces. That would have made the king only five years old when her father disappeared, and five was surely too young to be sending people on secret missions. But if her father was doing anything else on the island, he would have come home, or someone would have seen him sometime, somewhere, unless—

That thing that had been tickling her mind since last night suddenly caught hold of it: Unless he had been underground all this time, a captive to the Leafeaters. *Give me ten years in a room with one of them, and I assure you I wouldn't be able to teach him to say* please *to a beetle . . . he deserves to be whipped, scolded, hanged until he is thoroughly dead, and then sent to bed without supper . . .*

All her life, Persimmony had heard the name *Leafeaters* spat out like a curse by villagers who needed someone to blame for a lost spool of thread or a dead rooster. The first time she had ever seen them, she had been burying the dirty dishes under a tree at the edge of the woods. They were bent over large sacks, gliding silently between the trees. She had had an urge to follow them, but at that moment her mother had called out, "Persimmony, are those dishes clean yet?" and she had other problems to worry about. They were strange-looking people, she thought . . . not much taller than herself. Thin and pointy like branches, as if they were all thumbs and noses and knees and elbows, but with hair as soft as moss. Skin that was no color at all—or rather, it was as if all the colors in the world had gotten mixed together into a dull, muddy, gray mush spread sloppily over sharp bones. They loved the trees so much that they had come to look like them. Their green robes whispered when they walked, like the wind through the leaves—like wind and leaves telling secrets.

"Maybe he was in the woods saving someone from a tortoise," she mused aloud, "and the Leafeaters snuck up behind him and captured him. Or maybe he knew about someone else who had been kidnapped, and he somehow found the entrance to Willowroot and tried to rescue the person—but the Leafeaters surrounded him and locked him up in an underground prison cell. And he's been forced to eat pine needles ever since."

"Or, or, or," Worvil said excitedly, "maybe he did rescue the person, but on the way out he slipped and tumbled all the way down underground again and landed in an enormous pile of beetles." He was good at this game.

"Yes, and since the Leafeaters live underground, they love bugs, and were very angry with him for squashing any of them, and that's why they locked him away. I wonder if they were beetles or earthworms. Earthworms would be softer to land on, but more squashable. My mother once told me he tried to save the town of Candlenut from a swarm of angry cockroaches. But something went wrong, I think."

"Something always goes wrong," Worvil sighed.

Persimmony thought about what the Leafeaters had said last night. Gold buried under the mountain. A secret plot against the king. This wasn't a story in her head. This was a *real* adventure gathering around her—if only she could figure out what the adventure was, exactly. One thing she knew for certain: She had to find out where the two Leafeaters had gone and how to get down into their city. Somewhere underground might be a brave captive who had no idea—yet—that his daughter was brave enough to find him.

Suddenly there was a rustling behind her, and a stern voice said, "Persimmony, Persimmony, you naughty child! What will I do with you?"

Chapter 5

IN WHICH GEOGRAPHY TAKES A TURN FOR THE WORSE

King Lucas was one of those people who wanted to be known as wise but didn't particularly like to think. So he employed a professor to do his thinking for him and then tell him the interesting bits. It was difficult to hear those bits, though, while Guafnoggle, a Rumblebump who served as the king's jester, was cartwheeling across the throne room at top speed. Guafnoggle's long hair billowed out around him like a thick brown cloud, and his huge bare feet (which were even larger than Rumblebumps' feet usually are) thundered on the stone floor: boom BOOM . . . boom BOOM . . . boom BOOM . . .

"As you can see," yelled Professor Quibble over

the noise, "the island is entirely complete, with all forms of life known to humankind, all possible combination of plants, grasses, and soils, all the colors of the rainbow, nothing at all lacking anywhere, and— Oof! My eyeglasses!"

He was knocked off balance by the sudden lurching of the castle (the mountain had been particularly shaky as it rose this morning) and tumbled onto the map of the island that lay spread out on the floor of the throne room. Guafnoggle, who had landed upside down, rolled over and laughed.

Watching a Rumblebump's laughter is a little like getting caught in front of a tidal wave as it is about to break. Guafnoggle's laughter began as a twitching in his round, bulbous nose and spread first to his cheeks and then to his belly and then to his hands and his feet. Four buttons popped off his coat and went flying across the room. This was not too much of a loss since he was wearing at least three other coats underneath that one with plenty of buttons to spare.

The professor stood up again angrily, his eyeglasses returned a little crookedly to his nose. "Your Highness, for the hundredth time, must we put up with this? What good is a jester who laughs at *everything*? Geography is a serious subject."

Lucas, snickering in spite of himself, quickly

forced his face into a commanding frown. "Of course you're right, Professor. I was just about to say so myself. Guafnoggle, stop laughing!"

Guafnoggle stuffed the thick green and yellow folds of his coats into his mouth. He giggled as softly as he could until finally his laughter had ebbed into a gentle twitching in his nose and a slight trembling in his chin.

"As I was saying," continued the professor more calmly, "look to the north, the south, the east, the west . . . What do you see? Nothing but a great blue sea, stretching on and on forever. And so you can understand the high and noble role we must play, here at the Center of Everything. We are the last keepers of the Un-Blue Things. Without us, this earth would be an empty and colorless place!"

Even though Guafnoggle was sitting down now, when he spoke his words were still cartwheeling: "But how do you know the sea goes on and on forever on all sides, and how do you know the sky is blue behind your back when you aren't looking, because after all it might turn green or purple or orange the way the sunrise changes colors, and did you see how beautiful the sunrise was this morning?" Guafnoggle could never keep a sentence heading in a straight line and hated to slow down for punctuation unless absolutely necessary.

"The sea goes on and on forever," the professor said, gritting his teeth, "because there is no proof to the contrary, and if there is no proof to the contrary, then it is true."

"But how can you tell where the center is?" asked Lucas. "What's the center of forever?"

"Simple," answered Professor Quibble. "Wherever *we* are is the center."

"And the castle is in the center of the island."

"Well, more or less, since it is roughly in the middle of the mountain, which of course lies a little farther to the west than it does to the east, the Willow Woods stretching out quite far beyond its eastern side, so if we are going to be precise—"

"And my throne is in the center of the castle," continued Lucas.

"Er . . . of course, Your Highness."

"Aha! Then I *am* the center of the whole world! I knew it!" Lucas leaped to his feet.

Guafnoggle cried, "Don't get off the throne, Your Highness! You just threw the world off balance!"

Lucas sat down again quickly, but he had hardly spoken the words "proceed with the lesson" to

Professor Quibble when there was a banging on the north door of the throne room.

"Most likely it is someone from the digging team," said the professor.

"Oh, yes, I'd forgotten. HAROLD!" Lucas bellowed, and the south door opened with a groan, revealing a hunchbacked man holding a silver trumpet. "Harold! Visitors at the north door. Go announce them."

Harold hobbled across the throne room and disappeared behind the smaller north door. Five seconds later the door opened again, and there was a flourish of notes from the trumpet interrupted by a loud fit of coughing. "Dustin Dexterhoof, the royal (cough) archaeologist (cough, cough)."

Lucas strained his neck to see, but his visitor soon saved him the trouble. Dustin Dexterhoof emerged in front of the throne from a cloud of dirt and dropped on one muddy knee to kiss the king's hand.

"Long live the king," said the archaeologist. "I am your *humble* servant, *unworthy* of licking the dust from your shoes."

"They were clean until you came in," replied Lucas sourly, wiping his hand on his robes. "I hope this is important. You interrupted a very interesting geography lesson."

"I would not *dream* of bothering Your Highness with anything except the most *urgent* business. This is nothing short of a *dire emergency* requiring your *immediate* attention."

"Well then, what is it?"

"While obeying the king's command to search for the gold about which our *beloved* Lyre has prophesied, we have stumbled upon a most *unexpected, perplexing*, and in fact quite *disturbing* discovery. To come to the point—"

"Yes, why don't you?"

"—we have discovered gold—"

"Well, why didn't you say so in the first place? I knew the Lyre was telling the truth! Remember what it said?

A greater treasure lies below
Where rust and robbers cannot go,
And buried underneath your frown
A gold outshining any crown.

"So there *is* gold buried below! I'm rich!"

"You already were rich," said Guafnoggle. "Rich

as a king, rich as the sea, rich as a coffee cake, which I love, especially with seaweed piled on top."

Dustin Dexterhoof shifted his feet uncomfortably. "If Your Highness will allow me to finish—we *did* find gold. However, the gold unfortunately takes the *form* of, I mean to say, it has the *shape* of—to come to the point—a belt buckle."

The throne room was silent for a whole minute. King Lucas stared at Dustin Dexterhoof as if he were a moldy piece of cheese. "Do you mean to say," he said quietly, "that I have had all my dungeons dug up for the sake of a golden *belt buckle*?"

"If it makes you feel any better, Your Highness, it is quite a large belt buckle."

"How large?"

"Very large."

"HOW LARGE?"

"As big as the entire castle."

This time the throne room was silent for two minutes. Then Professor Quibble began to laugh hysterically. He laughed until his sides shook and the tears poured down and fogged up his eyeglasses. His laughter set Guafnoggle laughing, which set King Lucas laughing.

"Why, that is the most perpendicular thing I've ever heard!" gasped Lucas.

"*Preposterous,*" corrected the professor in between gulps.

"That too!"

Dustin Dexterhoof turned very red. "If you will follow me to the dungeon, Your Highness, you can see for yourself."

Lucas stopped laughing. "I'm the king! Kings don't go into their own dungeons. Get back to your digging."

Dustin Dexterhoof bowed and turned even redder. "I was afraid you would say that, Your Highness, and so *please* forgive me, for I have no choice—" He suddenly reached up, grabbed the crown from the king's head, and took off running toward the north door.

It took several seconds for Lucas to recover from the shock enough to yell, "How *dare* you!" and take off running after his crown, followed closely by the professor and Guafnoggle.

They ran out the north door, through the courtyard, down a staircase, through several long corridors, down another staircase, and over several sleeping diggers, until they finally bumped into Dustin Dexterhoof at the very bottom. Lucas angrily yanked his crown out of the archaeologist's hands, rammed it back on his forehead, and then looked out over a river of gold.

He pushed aside the sweaty men with shovels and dove onto the smooth surface. But though he tried to brush away the dirt and pry the gold up with his fingers, he could find no edge.

The archaeologist pulled a large piece of parchment from his pocket and spread it out in front of Lucas. "This is a diagram of the digging site in the dungeon," he explained. "This"—he drew his finger around a dark square taking up the entire digging site and a thinner line running through the middle of the square—"is the golden *object,* and within the outer square we have discovered not gold, not dirt, but *leather."*

"A belt?" sputtered the professor, choking on his own laughter.

"An enormous belt?" giggled Lucas.

"A *giant's* belt," said the archaeologist, raising one eyebrow significantly and rolling up the parchment again.

Lucas looked at him blankly, for he had never read any fairy tales. "Giant? What is a giant?"

"A very, very, very, very, very big person. Bigger than this castle. As big as a mountain, in fact."

"Are you actually suggesting that, hundreds of years ago, before this castle was built, a very big person passed by our island and accidentally left his belt?"

"No," replied Dustin Dexterhoof. "I am suggesting that he is *still here.*"

"There is a giant on this mountain?"

"*Under* this mountain," said Dustin Dexterhoof. "In fact, the giant *is* the mountain—or, in other words, the mountain *is* the giant—covered by a layer of dirt, of course. To come to the point, Your Highness, you are *at this very moment* standing on a giant's stomach."

Lucas looked down uneasily and stood on his tiptoes.

"All right, this joke has gone far enough," said Professor Quibble impatiently. "Stop wasting the king's time and get back to your digging. There is no such thing as a giant."

"What makes the mountain rise and fall, if not the breathing in and out of a giant buried beneath it?" asked the archaeologist.

"That is what mountains *do*," snapped the professor. "They are tied to the sun by an invisible string and therefore they rise and fall. It is an observable fact."

"*This* mountain rises and falls. But have you ever observed any other mountains?"

"Don't be silly. There are no other mountains. And besides, do you mean to tell me that a big person has been sleeping underground all this time without eating anything?"

"Perhaps he's *hibernating*, like a bat or a squirrel. Their breathing becomes very slow and they sleep for a long time without food."

"But this 'giant' would have been hibernating for hundreds and hundreds of years, long before the castle was built!"

"Which is why the dirt and grass gradually covered him up."

"And the mountain only rises and falls once a day. One breath a day? That's scientifically suspicious."

"Stop! Stop!" Lucas said. "You are both giving me a headache. There is to be no more talk of belt buckles or giants that don't exist. If there were a giant on this island, don't you think someone would have seen it?"

"I don't know. I'm only an archaeologist," said the archaeologist. "May I suggest that the king ask the *historian*?"

"The what?"

"The historian. He keeps all of the records of anything that has been done in the kingdom. He lives in the library."

Lucas was curious to meet this strange castle resident whom he had never seen. And so they climbed back over the sleeping diggers, went up the staircase, around the corner, down many more corridors and up many more staircases until they finally reached the library.

Chapter 6

In Which Persimmony Builds Castles and the Potter Makes Plans

Worvil and Persimmony both jumped at the sound of the voice behind them in the Willow Woods. Persimmony looked up and saw a halo of white hair and long fingers gripping a wooden cane. "Oh, Theodore! I was coming to find you, but I got lost and was almost eaten by a tortoise. This is Worvil. He was going to help me find my way home, but a tree ran away with his house."

Theodore smiled knowingly. "Ah, those restless mangroves. They're young still. Someday they'll find their way back to the shore and settle down in the water among the old ones, but for now they prowl around playing tricks on the tortoises and making life more difficult for everyone else. Come, my cottage is only a short distance to the west. I'll make you some breakfast."

This was not the first time the old potter had gotten Persimmony out of trouble. Years ago when she had decided to run away from home and become a fisherwoman on the Northern Shore, he had found her halfway through the woods, fed her a warm meal of lentil soup and cocoa, and convinced her gently that she would hate the smell of dead fish. From then on, Persimmony had gone often to the potter's cottage while her mother was in town, to read his books and listen to him tell stories of the old days when he had lived in the castle and dined with kings.

It was Theodore who had somehow known, without being told, that business was bad for Persimmony's mother. When other basket makers on the island began to dye their creations in bright colors and weave ribbons and flowers into them, suddenly Mrs. Smudge found herself left with a disturbing lack of customers. "We make plain, simple baskets," she had said to her daughters one evening after explaining why there was no food on the table. "No frills. I have a moral objection to frills." Prunella nodded sadly. Persimmony's stomach growled.

The next morning a clay pot had appeared on their doorstep. A plain, simple pot, with no frills—except that every day when they reached into it they pulled out a fresh, warm loaf of bread. This was the pot Persimmony accidentally broke with the broom.

The potter had built his cottage around the trunk of a willow tree after freeing it from the tortoise that lived there. (Theodore had lived in the forest for a great many years, and he was one of the few human beings for whom poison-tongued jumping tortoises had any respect.) A few feet away from the tree, in a clearing, stood a brick oven used for firing pottery. Around it on the grass were finished pots of all shapes and sizes.

One caught Persimmony's eye as she passed by with Theodore and Worvil. It had a cluster of clay leaves around its base and a wide, elegant neck. Oh, to have such a pot! What beautiful gift would come out of that?

She cast one longing glance at it before following the potter past the long willow branches tied back like curtains and through the door of the cottage. Inside the tiny dwelling, surrounded by the shelves of books, the mounds of clay, the potter's wheel, and a basket full of dirty smocks, Theodore served his guests a simple, comforting breakfast of warm oatmeal and cinnamon.

Theodore and Worvil ate at the table. Persimmony paced up and down the length of the cottage, holding the bowl of oatmeal in her hand and munching while she paced. She told her friend about the broken Giving Pot, her misadventures in the woods, and the Leafeaters' plans to dig through Mount Majestic and find the gold.

If she had been paying attention, she would have noticed a change come over the potter as she described the Leafeaters' conversation. He slowly stopped eating and sat hunched over, staring hard at the table, as if he were trying to decipher a message there. His lips moved silently.

"Well?" she finally concluded, placing her bowl on the table. She sat down on the floor and picked up a lump of the potter's clay. "What do you think?"

"I think that you should no longer throw brooms or go to the woods during a thunderstorm," replied Theodore.

"But what do you think about the Leafeaters?"

"Ah," sighed Theodore, standing up. He began absentmindedly clearing the dishes off the table, whisking away Worvil's half-eaten oatmeal while Worvil was scooping out another steaming hot spoonful. "I think we must go to the king and tell him immediately about the digging."

Persimmony frowned and punched a giant dimple in the handful of clay she was molding. "I was afraid you were going to say that."

"But then the Leafeaters would be angry at us!" mumbled Worvil, his mouth full of oatmeal. "What if they found us and took revenge?" He had already grown quite comfortable in the potter's cozy cottage.

But Persimmony's mind was racing. The three of them could find the gold first, give a third to the Leafeaters as a ransom for her father, give another third to the king as a show of undying loyalty to the crown, and keep a third to spread around the kingdom secretly. They would become heroes—and no one need know that the gold was ever divided up. Of course, she considered, they'd keep a third for themselves as well. She wondered how much that would leave them.

"And how, my child, do you propose that we find this gold?" asked Theodore when Persimmony had told him her scheme.

"Oh, I've already thought of that. We'll go to the castle at night, drug the gatekeeper, steal the keys, sneak down to the king's dungeons while the diggers are all fast asleep, and find the gold first."

"Daring, but it won't work. There are guards inside the castle. They have swords, and we have . . . pots." Theodore cocked one eyebrow at her in amusement, but his hands were busy stuffing cloaks and various items from his cottage into a small sack.

"Okay, okay, I have another idea."

"And what is that? Let me guess. I'll make a pot that will produce three huge shovels and we'll pick a spot on the side of the mountain and start digging ourselves."

"Well, it *could* work," she insisted, dropping another lump of clay on her knees.

"Persimmony!"

"But then the king would be angry at us!" Worvil

moaned. "He'll find out, and he'll have us all hung upside down by our toenails!"

"We must tell the king," Theodore repeated.

"What would be the point of warning him? It isn't his gold. The Leafeaters aren't exactly doing anything wrong."

"One way or the other," said Worvil, "someone is going to get angry at us, and I want to live with as few people angry at me as possible." He paused for a moment. "When you come right down to it, I just want to *live*."

"Trust me, Persimmony," said Theodore. "My dear, what *have* you done with all of my clay?"

Persimmony looked down. From the tips of her toes to her waist, she had covered herself with a mountain of clay. On top was a lumpy sort of castle, with clay towers standing crookedly out of the roof. Her legs felt cool and moist and safe underneath. She wriggled her toes and lifted up her knees slowly until the castle crumbled and the mountain cracked and fell apart in chunks. Her dress was now quite grimy.

She was secretly pleased with the fact that Theodore's plan meant that she, Persimmony Smudge, was going to go to the castle and meet the king face-to-face. No one she knew had ever actually *seen* the king. She had expected the potter to send her home.

"If your mother didn't have such a moral objection to reading," he sighed, "we could send her a note telling her where you are. As it is, we'll have to ask the king to send a messenger to her once we get to the castle. We can't waste time going all the way back to your cottage. We need to get started immediately. Come along, Worvil. Both of you heard the Leafeaters' plans, and it might take two witnesses to convince the king. He *must* believe us."

Worvil, horrified at the idea of facing the king, was hiding under the potter's bed. No amount of pleading or reasoning would convince him to come out, though Persimmony spent nearly half an hour on her hands and knees trying. "Okay," she said finally, hearing the potter's cane tapping impatiently at the door. "I understand. You can stay right here in the potter's cottage. Go ahead. It's much nicer than all your other houses. Of course, we might be gone for a very long time—days, weeks even. You never know with kings. And this is a *willow* tree. I bet the poison-tongued jumping tortoise who used to live here misses its home a lot. I certainly hope it doesn't think the potter has moved out for good, and come back to reclaim its tree one night. But don't worry—

you'll be asleep anyway, and you'll never feel its tongue. You won't even know you're dead."

Worvil's wide eyes suddenly appeared at the edge of the bed. "All right, all right! I'll come!" Persimmony clapped her hands, though she felt a little guilty at the same time. She dragged Worvil out, still shaking in fear, and the three set off.

As she followed the potter through the woods, Persimmony tried to remember the voices she had heard last night. "The Leafeaters seemed pretty angry at the king," she said out loud, "not to mention the Sunspitters, whoever they are."

"The Sunspitters are you and me," said Theodore, smiling. "All of us who live aboveground. All who are not Leafeaters. In their minds, we dishonor all that is beautiful and dignified—we spit at the sun." He paused, looking carefully at the trees and sniffing the air. "It has been so many years since I made this trip to this castle. Yes, due west. This way."

Persimmony was trying to be patient as they picked their way slowly along. The elderly potter with his stooped back and his cane did not move quickly, no matter how urgent the mission was, and they had to stop often to let him catch his breath. Meanwhile Worvil was dragging his feet with every step, whimpering softly to himself and jumping with fright every time a squirrel or lizard darted across his path. It gave her plenty of time to think. "What did we ever do to them?"

"A long time ago," the potter said, breathing hard, "the Leafeaters lived aboveground too. They were considered a very wise people, and kings and queens sought out their counsel before making any important decisions. But after the death of King Mumford the Modest, things changed. The rulers got richer and richer, and the people no longer cared about traditions and ceremonies and codes of courtesy and all the things that were important to the Leafeaters. One day, the Leafeaters were performing the Ceremony of Perpetual Wisdom for the coronation of King Lewis the Lighthearted. The entire kingdom was gathered, and the Chief of the Leafeaters was right in the middle of twirling the royal crown around his finger seven times, when the king suddenly *laughed*. Well, you can imagine what an insult that was. To a Leafeater, a ceremony is perhaps the most serious occasion there is. Furious, they outlawed all laughter amongst themselves and built a secret city underground called Willowroot, where no one else would ever bother them. The poison-tongued jumping tortoises took over the Willow Woods after that."

Persimmony thought this sounded an awful lot like pouting in a corner. "I'm surprised they ever come up to the surface at all or go into the villages, if they hate us so much."

"Well, they do need things—things you can't get underground, like candle wax, or stockings that don't itch, or certain spices. I suppose that even to a Leafeater leaves get a bit tasteless after a while—I'm sure a little paprika can do wonders to an acorn stew."

"One of the Leafeaters said something about a Ceremony of Tears. What is that?"

"The Ceremony of Tears is one of their most important ceremonies. They spend an entire day weeping and collect all their tears in vessels. They believe their tears have healing powers."

"I wish I had some of that!" said Persimmony, thinking of all of the bruises and scrapes she managed to get while climbing trees when she was supposed to be helping her mother. "I'd drink it every day."

"No, you wouldn't," said Theodore. "If you or I were to drink the Leafeaters' tears, we would be left speechless. We would not be able to say a single word."

"Forever?" said Persimmony, shocked.

"No." The potter laughed gently. "For a few days, depending on how much we drank. But for *some* people, to lose one's voice even for an hour would be a tragedy worse than death!"

Persimmony chose to ignore this. "How do you know all this?"

"Books, my dear, books! You can learn a lot by reading."

Persimmony sighed. Ever since she had heard about the gold, she had dreamed of all the books she could buy at the market, books full of adventures beyond what she could imagine on her own. "And do your books say anything about gold under the mountain?"

"No, but they have told me other things—things that make me certain we cannot keep this news of the Leafeaters' plans to ourselves."

"What things?"

But Theodore did not answer. Instead, he asked, "My child, why do you want this gold so badly?"

Persimmony blushed. "Well, I just thought maybe we could offer it to the Leafeaters in exchange for something we wanted—or someone—like a prisoner, maybe, that they had held captive for a long time—like, oh, seven years."

Theodore looked at her sadly for a moment. "If you want to know where your father is, Persimmony, you should have a talk with your mother."

"Well, I have, but all she says is—" Persimmony looked at him suspiciously. "Why? Do you know something?"

"Oh my, look how high the sun is getting! We've got to hurry, and here I am wasting my breath with talking. Worvil, keep up!"

"Theodore!"

But the potter had aimed his cane to the west with fierce energy and was wheezing loudly as he picked up the pace. Persimmony, surprised into silence, followed him.

Chapter 7

IN WHICH A SMUDGE GETS A GOOD WASHING

I was deep in thought in the royal library and putting the finishing touches on my latest book, *A Brief History of Famous People Eaten by Poison-Tongued Jumping Tortoises*, when the door swung open with a loud bang and a shower of dust. King Lucas, Professor Quibble, Dustin Dexterhoof, and Guafnoggle squeezed in among the piles of books and papers and maps.

"Greetings, Your Highness," I said, surprised.

"Why have I never seen you before?" Lucas demanded, taking in my shabby clothes and ink-stained hands with one sweeping glance.

"Because you have never summoned me before. And neither did your father, I might add." I did

not add that his father, King Lionel the Lofty, was a haughty and heartless man, who never shed a tear when his wife died in childbirth, who once had all the flowers on the island plucked and burned after a bouquet made him sneeze, and whose face was now painted on doormats in the villages and decorated with muddy footprints. I have found that

most kings don't want to know *that* much history.

"Then you must be a very unimportant person," said Lucas.

"So I've been told, Your Highness," I replied sadly.

"But the archaeologist insists that you may be able to help us answer an annoying question. Has anyone ever seen a giant under Mount Majestic?"

"Why, yes," I said.

Professor Quibble, who had been absently thumbing through an atlas, looked up sharply. Dustin Dexterhoof stifled a smile. The king stared at me. "*Yes?*"

"It says so in your father's diary. All royal diaries end up in the library eventually, and it is my job to read them, if you'll excuse me."

"My *father* knew about a giant?"

"He knew about a *report* of a giant. Seven years ago, a peppercorn picker apparently came to him claiming to have discovered the head of a giant in a cave on the Western Shore."

Guafnoggle laughed in delight. "The Snoring Cave! The Snoring Cave! It was a giant snoring and we never knew—how funny, how marvelous, oh, wait until I tell the others!"

"Wait a minute, wait a minute. What Snoring Cave?" asked King Lucas. "And what was a peppercorn picker doing on the Western Shore to begin with? No wonder I keep running out of pepper."

Guafnoggle was climbing over stacks of historical records. "The Rumblebumps have always called it the Snoring Cave, but we never go inside because it is so long and dark and far away from the water, and of course we hate anything long and dark and far away from the water, and all these years we thought it was an underground wind that made that sound!"

"What sound?"

"Well, a sound a little like a growl and a little like the rain beating down on the rocks in a storm and a little like a very hungry stomach and a little like thunder and a whole lot like a snore."

"Here," I said, reaching for one particular book on the top shelf and flipping through the pages. "Listen for yourself."

Thursday. Nothing much happened today. I ate lobster for lunch, rearranged the portraits in the great hall, and washed a peppercorn picker's mouth out with soap. The last was especially bothersome. He had the nerve to come to me, sweaty and red-faced, blabbering something about a giant's head in one of the caves. A giant! People who read fairy tales are never up to any good. And so I gave him the soap punishment for lying. Then I told him he is never under any circumstances to mention such a lie to anyone, or he would be locked in the dungeon and his family would be forced to eat nothing but soap until they all perished from extreme cleanliness. There, that is done. Let whoever finds this diary forever smudge out the memory of that ridiculous name SIMEON SMUDGE.

Despite his confusion, Lucas couldn't help feeling proud. He didn't remember very many things about his father, but if his father hadn't believed such a silly rumor about a giant, then he didn't need to either.

"I apologize for not following your father's wishes, Your Highness, but a historian never smudges anything out. However, according to the Candlenut town records, Simeon Smudge has not reported for work in seven years. In fact, he is listed as 'missing.'"

"And that's it? No one else has ever mentioned a giant?"

"Well, no one except Theodore the Wise, a potter who now lives in the Willow Woods. He was exiled from the castle eighty years ago—by your grandfather, in fact, who didn't appreciate the suggestion that there was anything bigger than himself in the world. If you ask *my* opinion—"

"I didn't," said Lucas.

"Of course not, Your Highness."

Professor Quibble's eyes opened wide. "The potter is still alive? He must be over a hundred years old. Your Highness, this is lucky indeed. Theodore the Wise discovered a way of making clay pots that produce whatever the owner asks."

"*Whatever* the owner asks?" Lucas smiled and thought of his pepper shaker. "Give the order for the Willow Woods to be searched and Theodore the Wise to be captured and brought to the castle immediately—along with his pots. And then tell the cook I'm hungry. There are too many staircases in this castle."

It was nearly noon by the time Persimmony, Worvil, and Theodore finally reached the grassy foot of Mount Majestic—and something else. Six armed soldiers bearing the royal crest were coming straight toward them, pulling a large wooden cart. "Halt!" barked the first soldier. "We are looking for Theodore the Wise, who lives in the Willow Woods. Can you tell us where to find him?"

"You've found him," said the potter, stepping forward.

Having been warned to expect trouble, the soldiers were not sure how to react to this. "Theodore the Wise," said the leader awkwardly, "we are, um, under direct orders from the king to escort you and your, uh, pottering stuff—to the castle immediately. If you resist, there will be, um, well, punishments beyond your worst nightmares."

Worvil fainted. "Good grief," said Persimmony, pinching and wiggling his nose until he woke up again. What could the king possibly want with

Theodore? Could he have heard about the Leafeaters' plot already from someone else? The potter simply shook his head, sighed, and patiently explained to the soldiers how to get to his cottage and where to find his pots. "Don't break any!" he warned. Three of the soldiers departed with their cart into the woods. The others surrounded Theodore, Persimmony, and Worvil to accompany them the rest of the way to the castle.

"The mountain is at its highest now," grumbled one of the soldiers. "Can't we wait until it sinks so we won't have to climb as far?"

"The king said *immediately*," said another, and the company began the difficult trek up the mountain.

Chapter 8

In Which Philosophy Leads to a Ticklish Conclusion

King Lucas *was in* the middle of a philosophy lesson. At the moment, Professor Quibble was busy getting into the correct posture, which he had to get exactly right in order to concentrate as a philosopher needed to do. First he bent one knee upward and rested the foot on his other leg. Then he held the bridge of his nose delicately between his thumb and forefinger and raised the other arm upward in a graceful curve like a half moon. "Now, where were we? Oh, yes. We were about to discuss the most ancient philosophical question: Which came first, the chicken or the egg?"

Philosophy required a lot of thinking, and it got tiring watching the professor think so much. So

King Lucas was happy to be interrupted by a trumpeting so loud and long and grand that the very walls of the throne room seemed to quake at the sound.

"Visitors!" he exclaimed. He jumped to his feet and straightened his crown before calling out in a deep and dignified voice, "You may enter."

The door opened and a nervous face peered into the throne room. "I'b sorry, your High-dess, but I was just blowing by dose." The young man's nose was as swollen and red as a tomato, and he held a large dirty handkerchief in his hand.

"What? Where's Harold?" Lucas demanded.

"Harold had to clead his trubpet. After de archaeologist cabe, it would dot play a dote. He sedt be to take his place. I hab a cowd." And he blew his nose again to demonstrate.

"I didn't understand a word of that. What is your name?"

"Badley, Your High-dess."

"Well, Badley—"

"Dot Badly," said the poor fellow, struggling to pronounce his consonants. "*Badley*. Eb, ay, ed, el, ee, why." (His name, of course, was really *Manley*, but unfortunately he has been called *Badly* ever since.)

"That's what I said! Badly, I forbid you to blow

your nose unless you are announcing visitors. It is very confusing."

"Yes, Your High-dess."

After the young man disappeared, King Lucas sighed and climbed back onto the throne again. "I was so hoping it would be Theodore with the pots that will give me whatever I want. I want pepper. There's nothing in the world better than pepper."

"Which brings us to our next philosophical question." The professor smiled, striking the correct pose just in time to save the conversation. "Is something good because it is good for *me*, or because it is good for *you*?" He was cut short by another blast of trumpeting. Professor Quibble fell into a heap on the floor and put his head in his hands.

"Badly!" yelled Lucas as the door opened. "I'll cut off your nose if you do that again!"

But this time Badly was not alone. He was followed by an old man leaning on a cane and a girl who was just about the dirtiest person Lucas had ever seen (except for the archaeologist, of course). An odd-looking man, crouched close to the floor, came in last. "Theodore de potter, Persibbody SssM-MMMnnggggPHPHPH"—(Badly buried his face in his handkerchief to stifle a sneeze)—"de basket baker's daughter, add Worvil de . . . er . . . de worrier."

Lucas rose to his feet and spread out his arms in welcome. "Come in! Come in! It is an honor to have Theodore the Wise and his assistants in the castle. You will be my guests for as long as you wish to stay."

Persimmony marched straight into the throne room, ready to save the world—as soon as she found out what to save it from. In the midst of so much finery she realized how filthy she must look. Her dress was ripped from her race through the forest in a thunderstorm, she was covered with dried mud from her night in the hollow tree trunk, there were leaves stuck in her hair and clay stuck under her fingernails, and she couldn't remember the last time she'd had a bath. Well, there was nothing to do but pretend she was clean. She stepped toward the king. "I'm so pleased to meet—"

Lucas ignored her. "I hope your journey was pleasant," he said to Theodore, "and that your—belongings—have arrived safely as well?" He laughed nervously and pushed up his crown.

"Your Highness, there is not a moment to lose," said Theodore, still wheezing from his climb up the mountain. "The kingdom may be in peril."

Lucas rolled his eyes. "I suppose you're going to tell me about the giant."

The potter was not expecting this. "You know about the giant?"

"Giant? What giant?" said Persimmony. Behind her she could hear Worvil mumbling under his breath, "Good day, Your Highness . . . I am your loyal servant . . . I have never met these two people in my life . . . You're looking remarkably well . . . May I kiss your hand? . . . I'm allergic to dungeons . . . Treason? I would never dream of it . . ." Since the newcomers had arrived, Guafnoggle had begun poking Worvil, trying to decide whether he was a man or a very large jellyfish. When Theodore said the word "peril," however, Worvil broke free and threw himself at the king's feet.

"I confess! I confess!" he sobbed. "I didn't want to come and tell you. But I'll tell you now. I'll tell you everything."

"Your Highness," Persimmony said, "Worvil is not quite himself right now. Well, actually, he *is* himself, unfortunately. But you'd better let me start from the beginning."

"Tell me what?" Lucas asked suspiciously, trying to free his robes from Worvil's hands.

Worvil's words came pouring out. "Oh, the Leafeaters, the Leafeaters, they are a wicked and disloyal people. I would never do such a thing. The king's gold is the king's gold. Don't blame Persimmony—she just heard them talking. She's no traitor."

"What on earth is this mad little man saying?"

"Under the earth, they're under the earth," wailed Worvil.

Persimmony stamped her foot. "Will someone please *look* at me?"

And Lucas did, reluctantly, as if she were a cabbage. He hated cabbages.

Then Persimmony explained, from beginning to end, how she and Worvil had come to be hidden in a tree trunk in the middle of the night when the Leafeaters came out, and what they had overheard. By the time she finished, King Lucas had turned several different shades of purple. His mouth opened and closed, his hands clenched and unclenched themselves, and his nose twitched so much that Persimmony didn't know if he was going to cry or sneeze.

The visitors waited expectantly.

"How *dare* they?" Lucas finally burst out. "Traitors! Knaves! Villains! Conspirators! Double-crossing scoundrels!" He ran out of words and looked to the professor for help.

"Gold diggers?" the professor offered.

Guafnoggle suddenly began laughing and rolling around on the floor. "There's no gold but a belt buckle and nothing under the mountain but a giant! A giant belt, a giant buckle, a giant belt buckle!" he crowed.

"What *is* all this about a giant?" insisted Persimmony.

Lucas snorted. "The royal diggers found a golden belt buckle under the castle and think it belongs to a giant, and the historian says his head is in a cave on the Western Shore."

"The historian's head?"

"The *giant's* head."

"But that's ridiculous!"

"No, it isn't." The potter spoke with such conviction that everyone in the room turned to look at him. "I tried to tell your grandfather King Lugbar that very thing, and because no one listened to me, the entire island is now in imminent danger."

"Danger?" said Lucas. "In danger of what?"

"Of the giant waking up, of course."

Persimmony stared at her friend. "There's a giant— under the mountain?"

"Yes."

"But how do you know?"

"Before I was cast out of the castle, I had spent my whole life writing down and studying the prophecies of the Lyre-That-Never-Lies. I became convinced that the Lyre's words pointed to a startling conclusion: that there is a sleeping giant buried under Mount Majestic and that this giant will have a crucial role to play in the fate of the island." Theodore leaned heavily on his cane as though too weary to go on. "I hoped and hoped I was wrong, and finally I convinced myself that there was no giant after all. But now this news confirms it. And with the Leafeaters digging right toward him, I fear the worst."

"I don't understand," said Lucas, scratching his ear.

"Ahem! Perhaps I can help, Your Highness." Professor Quibble emerged from his quiet corner and came forward. "Will you allow me to expound the situation logically?"

"If that means you'll explain it so I can understand, please do."

"Very well, then," said the professor, happily returning to his posture of intense concentration. "*If* there is a giant (which is a very big IF), then his head lies on the western side of this island, near the caves of the Rumblebumps."

"The Snoring Cave!" said Guafnoggle, grabbing his feet and rocking back and forth.

"If his head is on the western side of the island," the professor continued, "then his feet must lie on the eastern side, since a person's feet are usually at the opposite end of the body from the head."

Lucas looked down at his toes and saw this to be true.

"If his feet are at the eastern end of Mount Majestic, then they lie at the edge of the Willow Woods, where the Leafeaters live."

"They live under the woods," said Persimmony.

"Naturally. And if the Leafeaters are digging toward the center of Mount Majestic from the direction of the Willow Woods, then they will be digging *straight into the giant's feet.*"

Lucas slumped down lower in the throne.

Professor Quibble was enjoying himself immensely. "If hundreds of shovels and pickaxes suddenly begin pricking and tickling the giant's feet, then he will surely wake up. If the giant wakes up and rises, then the entire mountain will erupt and crumble to the ground, causing unimaginable destruction below." The professor's lips curled upward in a smirk, and he lowered his voice. "We would all be like insects crushed under his heels. A being that big, if he existed, could eat a hundred brave men for breakfast and still have room for a barbecued whale or two. Therefore, if there is in fact a giant beneath Mount Majestic"—he paused

dramatically before delivering his final punch—
"we are in big trouble."

For a long time no one spoke.

"Maybe the giant is wearing shoes," offered Persimmony.

The potter shook his head. "I'm afraid we can't take that chance."

Lucas swung around to face the professor. "Don't tell me you suddenly believe this nonsense!"

The professor let out a loud snort. "As a philosopher, I'd say that it presents the very knotty problem of whether or not I should bother to eat breakfast tomorrow morning. But as a geographer, I'd say that I've never seen a single map of the island that mentioned a Snoring Cave or a giant. As a man of science, I would scoff at the very idea. And as a mathematician, adding one plus one plus one—one old potter plus one dirty archaeologist plus one crazy peppercorn picker—I'd have to say . . . No. I don't believe a word of it."

Lucas rose to his feet. "Follow me to the great hall. We shall see what the Lyre has to say."

Chapter 9

IN WHICH A LYRE
TELLS THE TRUTH
(PERHAPS)

The Lyre-That-Never-Lies has been a prized possession of the kings and queens of the Island at the Center of Everything since the earliest days of the monarchy. Some claim that it had once been an ordinary musical instrument in the hands of a common village musician until the Voice came and filled its strings with a music more lovely and more haunting than anything that had ever been heard before.

But people only believe what they want to believe.

The Lyre once told Queen Lulu the Luminous that her vanity would be her downfall. The queen shouted, "I don't believe it!" A week later her entire body turned bright green from all the skin creams she had put on it, and for the rest of her reign she never showed herself in public again. Behind her back she was called Queen Lulu the Ludicrous until her dying day.

As Lucas got down off the throne and walked past his guests with as much majesty as he could muster under the circumstances, he went over the Lyre's recent prophecy in his mind. He had been eager to believe that there was gold underneath the castle—but perhaps he had misinterpreted the Lyre's words. They were often hard to understand, after all.

A greater treasure lies below
Where rust and robbers cannot go,
And buried underneath your frown
A gold outshining any crown.

There was nothing about a giant in that. "Greater treasure" and "gold outshining any crown" didn't sound like a belt buckle.

Everyone followed him to the east end of the throne room and into the great hall, where the royal musician sat. She unlocked the golden clasp of an oak chest and lifted out a beautiful instrument, made of a small tortoise shell with two wooden arms sticking out of the top and a wooden crossbar in between. Strung between the crossbar and the tortoise shell were seven strings. The royal musician held the Lyre gently in her arms, then with a graceful movement she took a small seashell and drew it once across the strings.

A chord rang out, softly at first but swelling louder and louder. Then the words began from deep within the Lyre's music:

Buried fear will fly away;
Silent hands will speak;
The low will be the lofty,
And the strong will be the weak.

"So there *is* a giant!" said Persimmony, breaking the silence that followed.

"Don't be silly," retorted Lucas. "The Lyre never mentioned a giant."

"But he's buried! And he'll cause fear! I don't understand the bit about flying, though. Do giants have wings?"

"Of course not. And anyway, the Lyre said the strong will become weak, so that means even if there is a giant, which there isn't, he's going to be too weak to push his way out of the mountain. We have nothing to fear."

"I don't think that's what it means at all!"

"Doesn't matter. It's balderdribble anyway," said Lucas.

"Balder*dash*," said Professor Quibble.

"That too."

But the Lyre wasn't finished yet. It began to sing again:

It won't be long before His Royal Highness
Must learn to share the milk of human kindness.
And if to swallow pride he does not dare,
Beware!
Beware!

"Oh dear, oh dear!" cried Worvil, who up to this point had felt unusually calm and peaceful. But the word "beware" struck terror in his heart despite the beauty of the Lyre's music.

"That didn't sound right," said Lucas. "*Highness* and *kindness* don't rhyme."

"Maybe that's the point," said the potter.

"Well, whatever the point is, I don't believe it. There's no such thing as a giant. It's ludiculous! Ridiposterous! Insanitorious!"

The ringing of the Lyre stopped.

That night King Lucas held a secret conference with Professor Quibble, the captain of the castle guard, and Theodore. Persimmony and Worvil were not invited. Worvil was quite happy to go straight to sleep after supper, but Persimmony sat at the foot of her bed fuming.

"It's not fair!" she said to the ceiling of the guest chamber. She had been led to it several hours earlier and given strict orders to wash herself thoroughly before putting on the nightgown provided for her and getting into bed. It was the nicest, silkiest nightgown she'd ever seen in her life, but she didn't care. "I'm the one who overheard the Leafeaters' plans. I'm the one who reported the news to the king. And now I'm being left out of everything that really matters and sent to bed like I was being punished. It's not fair!"

Then she decided to do something about it.

The meeting was taking place in the king's private chambers. She knew because she had hidden in the shadows and followed the little group after supper to a large door with words of warning etched into the wooden surface: "KING'S PRIVATE CHAMBERS. NO ADMITTANCE. KEEP OUT. YES, THAT MEANS YOU." A soldier had been stationed outside the door, but now as she tiptoed back down the dark hallway she found the soldier slouched against the wall, fast asleep.

Persimmony pressed her ear to the door and strained to listen. Immediately, she recognized Theodore's voice.

"No, no, it will never do to send the soldiers

alone," he was saying. "Why, the ones you sent before haven't even returned with my pots yet! No one knows the underground city's entrances. I'm telling you, you must let Persimmony and me lead them. Persimmony said she heard the Leafeaters' voices disappear quickly—the tree trunk where she was hiding must have been near one of their entrances. She can find it again, I'm sure of it, and I can keep us from getting lost."

"Don't be a fool, old man. Of course the king isn't going to let you go." It was Professor Quibble. "We need your pots. We need you to make more, if necessary. We aren't going to let a prize like you out of our grasp."

Theodore shook his head sadly. "If you sent your soldiers to capture me because you heard my pots will give you whatever you want, I'm sorry to say that you have been misinformed."

"Do you mean you *refuse* to obey your king?" Lucas demanded.

"I mean I *cannot* do the thing you want. I will tell you the same thing I told your grandfather: I have no control over what comes out of my pots. I simply make them. What comes out is what people *need*, not what they want."

"Well, I need pepper. I need lots of it. Immediately. And after that, I need swords and axes and bows and arrows and daggers for my war against the Leafeaters."

"I can guarantee that my pots will not give you any of those things."

"Don't you realize that I could have you arrested for treason?"

"It will not be the first time," said the potter quietly. "Please listen to me. You must make peace with the Leafeaters, apologize for whatever wrongs you may have done them, and offer amends. Only then do we have any hope of warning them about the giant."

"For the last time, there is no giant. This is a battle and we will punish them for their rebellion. Captain Gidding has already been told to spare no one. Right, Captain Gidding?"

The only response was a soft snore.

"The Leafeaters are stubborn," sighed the potter, "but I'm confident they will listen if we come to them with courtesy instead of with weapons. Let me go and talk to them, with Persimmony's help to find the entrance, and the soldiers behind us to protect us if need be."

Lucas snorted. "Ha! A poor, grimy basket maker's daughter with hair the color of cold porridge and no idea how to curtsy properly? Leading the royal troops? Crazy. Give her a broom and let her make herself useful by sweeping the pantry floor."

Persimmony flung open the door to the king's chambers and stormed into the room. "You are the rudest, meanest, shortest, and *selfishest* king I have ever met in my life and I wouldn't curtsy to you if you paid me the sun and moon and every star in the sky to do it! I hope the giant wakes up and topples your precious mountain to pieces!"

Everyone in the room jumped and stared—well, everyone except for Captain Gidding, who was still snoring.

Lucas rose to his feet in fury. "This is a private meeting! How dare you enter uninvited?"

"How dare you not invite me?"

"How dare you talk back to the king?"

"How dare you talk at all?"

"I'll send you to the dungeon!" Lucas screamed.

"Um, Your Highness," whispered Professor Quibble. "Have you forgotten that your dungeon is an archaeological dig at present?"

"Oh, yes," Lucas said, and he thought for a moment. "I'll send you to the *library*!"

Persimmony crossed her arms. "Go ahead. I like reading."

Lucas opened his mouth, and then shut it again

and sat down with a scowl on his face. "*You* are an annoying girl," he said after a pause.

"*You* . . ." Persimmony began. She was going to say, "*You* are a rotten king," but Theodore caught her eye and gave her a look of warning. "*You* . . . are wearing your crown backward," she said, and sat down in the middle of the floor with her chin propped in her hands.

Lucas's hands flew to his crown and twisted it around on his head.

Professor Quibble coughed and raised his eyebrows at the king. "If I were you, Your Highness," he said, "I would silence these rumors about the giant once and for all."

"How?" asked Lucas grumpily.

"By sending someone to this so-called Snoring Cave—a witness to prove that there is no giant there."

"Good idea. I'll send Guafnoggle tomorrow."

Professor Quibble coughed. "No offense to your, er, delightful jester, but do you remember the last time you asked him to do something for you? The *blueberry pie* incident? There is a permanent purple stain on the ceiling of the armory, and to this day apparently the children of Bristlebend scream every time they see a spatula."

"Oh." Lucas cringed. "We'll need someone to go with him then. I don't suppose—?"

"Don't look at me," said the professor. "I have far too much to think about right now. But someone who is otherwise unoccupied . . ." He stared hard at the king and winked.

"You're not suggesting that *I* go?"

"Of course not, Your Highness. But if some person"—he coughed again—"is in need of some form of amusement outside the castle"—he winked several more times—"to keep out of trouble . . ." He leaned his head slightly in Persimmony's direction.

"What? Aaaaaaahhh." Lucas's eyes lit up. "Why yes, Professor, you're exactly right." He turned back to Persimmony. "I hereby name you Royal Giant Hunter. Tomorrow you will go with Guafnoggle to the Western Shore, find the Snoring Cave, and look inside it. If there's a giant there"—he snickered—"come back and tell me immediately. If not, you are free to go home to your mother. And to conclude this meeting—"

"Wait a minute!" Persimmony sputtered. She wanted to be going east with the soldiers to the Willow Woods. She wanted to face the Leafeaters and save the kingdom and find her father, who she imagined was nearly dying of boredom in some secret underground cell in Willowroot, counting tree roots and tying centipedes into necklaces. She couldn't bear the thought that anyone else would find him but her.

"To conclude this meeting," Lucas said more loudly, turning away from Persimmony, "I forbid any more discussion of the so-called giant. No one in the kingdom needs to hear any silly rumors about a giant under the mountain. Is that clear?"

"No, it is *not* clear," cried Persimmony. She looked to the potter for help, but Theodore was looking thoughtfully down at his cane. Why wouldn't he stick up for her?

"What about the small fellow—the worrier?" said the professor. "You don't want him hanging around the castle with that stupid, The-World-Is-About-to-End look on his face."

"No," Lucas groaned. "We could send him back to the woods, but he won't be useful to the soldiers. He's scared of his own shadow."

"He is not!" Persimmony said hotly. "He's just scared of everyone *else's* shadow."

"I suppose we'll have to find a corner of the dungeon where no one is digging and keep him there till this is over."

Persimmony was horrified at such cruelty. "Worvil may be little," she cried, "but he thinks big. He'll probably be a hero someday. So there!"

"Well then, if he's going to be a hero, you'll certainly need him," Lucas said. "He can go with you to the Western Shore."

"But—"

"It's all settled, then," Lucas interrupted. "Theodore the Wise will stay in the castle and make pots. Captain Gidding will lead the soldiers in battle against the Leafeaters. And Persimmony and Worvil will accompany Guafnoggle to the Snoring Cave tomorrow. Now I'm going to bed." Putting both hands over his ears, he walked across the room through a door on the other end and closed it behind him.

Persimmony returned to her chamber furious. She washed her face with one of the lace curtains, put the silky nightgown on backward, and went to sleep with her head at the foot of the bed and her dirty feet on the fluffy white pillows.

Chapter 10

In Which the King's Empty Pepper Shaker Results in Tyranny, Oppression, and a General Unsettling of the Nose

While Persimmony, Theodore, Worvil, and Lucas had been busy arguing, planning, and worrying, Persimmony's mother and sister had been frantically searching for her in the woods.

They did not find Persimmony, of course, but they did find someone else—or rather, he found them.

It was early afternoon on the day after the thunderstorm before Mrs. Smudge sat down to rest on a large rock, fanning herself with a leaf and bemoaning the disobedience of her lost child. Prunella lay on the ground because her feet hurt so badly.

All at once, Prunella felt a strong rope being wrapped around her. As she was swung over a man's shoulder, she caught a glimpse of his pinched nose and despicable grin. "What are you doing?" she gasped, too shocked even to scream.

"We are kidnapping you, of course," said Mr. Fulcrumb, the foreman of the king's pepper mill.

"But—but that isn't *nice*," said Prunella.

Mrs. Smudge struggled furiously against the rope that held her to the bony back of the foreman's assistant. "Don't just hang there, Prunella. Call for help! *HEEEELLLLLLLLLLLLP!!!*"

"But there's no one around to hear us!" wailed her daughter.

"That's exactly right," snickered Mr. Fulcrumb. "And no one would help you anyway. I've found twenty-eight new workers for the pepper mill this very morning, and you two lovely ladies are the icing on the cake."

Prunella gazed in horror at the back of the foreman's knees, which was all she could see of him. "You're going to *eat* us?"

When their two captors only laughed, Mrs. Smudge sank her teeth into the closest part of the assistant's body she could reach—which put a quick stop to the laughing, but not to the kidnapping.

Along the southern and southwestern borders
of the woods, near the Smudges' cottage, the trees
grew more sparsely and were covered with pepper
vines twisting up their trunks. The pepper mill was
an ugly, tall, round stone structure farther to the
west, just outside of Candlenut. It had a door on one
side where the workers went in and a chute on the
other side where the newly ground pepper came

spewing out into big wooden carts to be taken to the castle.

Mrs. Smudge was livid and Prunella was weeping loudly when Mr. Fulcrumb and his assistant untied their hands and pushed them through the mill's shadowy entrance. As soon as her hands were free the basket maker smacked the foreman across the face. "If you think I'm going to go one step further into this evil place, you are two quacks short of a roast duck. Let me and my daughter go immediately."

"Ah, I would, I would, my good woman, but you see it is not I, but the king, who has requested your presence in this fine establishment. Spare the pepper and spoil the soup, you know."

"Don't you go quoting your crooked proverbs to me. It's the rotted tree that catches the fire, I say!"

"Don't bite the hand that keeps you out of prison."

"Those who live in stone towers shouldn't throw glasses!"

"Misery loves company."

Mrs. Smudge opened her mouth and shut it again. Then she smoothed out her contorted face and folded her hands demurely in front of her. "I'm afraid I cannot be of service to you," she said calmly.

"Why not?" demanded Mr. Fulcrumb.

"I have a moral objection to physical labor."

"Then I hope you have no moral objection to dungeons, because that's where you will be after you have been convicted of treason against the king. You *and* your pretty daughter."

Prunella stared at him. "Mother, please, please do what he says!"

Mrs. Smudge sucked in her outrage and crossed her arms across her chest tightly, but her nostrils turned bright red. She followed Mr. Fulcrumb up the flight of stairs that lay just inside the entrance of the mill, kicking each step with her toe as she went and muttering under her breath.

Mr. Fulcrumb's voice echoed above their heads. "You should be honored to be a part of such an important service to your king. Many hands make more pepper, you know."

"No, it's 'Many hands make more baskets'! You always twist everything for your purposes! This is what comes of education. The more people think, the more they think up cruel things to do to other people. This is what my Persimmony will become, filling her head with books and dreaming of doing everything except what she was born and raised to do—making fine baskets, keeping a clean house, and putting bread on the table. Oh, Prunella, my poor lamb, my pretty puppet, whatever shall become of you? You are too young and beautiful to be slaving away in a pepper mill." This time she caught the foreman's heel with her toe.

Mr. Fulcrumb quickened his pace. "Save your breath, woman. You'll be needing it when we get to the top."

They certainly had little breath left when they reached the top of the staircase that spiraled its way around the inner wall of the mill. At first Mrs. Smudge and her daughter thought the mill was on fire, for the large room at its summit was thick with smoke. But the smoke was actually the fine, dusty residue of the pepper grinder in the center of the room. A huge vat sat on top of a wooden contraption with thick beams jutting out around it like spokes on a wheel. Lined up along each beam were several workers pushing it—men, women, and children. Mrs. Smudge stared anxiously at each child that passed by, but none was Persimmony.

Prunella sneezed. Mr. Fulcrumb handed her and Mrs. Smudge each a wooden clothespin. Puzzled, they looked at him and saw that he had taken another clothespin (this one made of gold) out of his pocket and put it on his nose. Then they realized that all of the people in the mill had wooden clothespins on their noses to keep from sneezing. So they did the same.

"That beab is yours," said Mr. Fulcrumb, pointing to one empty beam in the turning wheel. He sounded a little less dignified with his nostrils pinched together, but no one was in the mood to laugh. He turned to the rest of the workers and bellowed, "FASTER! FASTER, YOU LAZY WEAKLIGS, OR YOU'LL BE SEEIG THE IDSIDE OF THE ROYAL DUD-GEODS TOBORROW!" Then he went back down the stairs, leaving them to their fate. His assistant silently stood guard by the door.

"Bay your sleep be full of dightbares and your bed be full of bosquitoes!" yelled Mrs. Smudge, but a moment later she was nearly flattened by five men coming up the stairs carrying huge sacks on their shoulders. The men mounted a platform that extended over the heads of the workers at the grinder and stopped just above the vat. They poured in pounds and pounds of peppercorns, dried black in the sun, from the storerooms beside the mill. Then they returned and trudged down the stairs again to gather more. Mrs. Smudge looked after them for a long time. Her husband had been a peppercorn picker too. He had climbed these very stairs and dumped his sack into that horrible hole. "Oh, by poor lost Sibeod," she whispered. "What you had to put up with!"

She and Prunella took their places at their assigned beam and began to push.

Supper was a slice of stale bread and a cup of lukewarm water. (Mr. Fulcrumb kept all the good food for himself.) The drudgery continued until midnight, when a bell rang and the workers returned to their homes—everyone except the Smudges, who stumbled into the fresh night air, took off their clothespins, breathed deeply, found a patch of soft grass, and fell sound asleep under the full moon, dreaming of Persimmony and baskets and their own beds.

Chapter 11

IN WHICH OUR HEROES ARE ARMED WITH MIGHTY WEAPONS AND MANY PANCAKES ARE CONSUMED

Very well, then, she would prove there was a giant.

That was Persimmony's first thought when she woke up the next morning with a sore neck but a clearer mind. She took her feet off the fluffy royal pillows (pleased to see the dirty footprints they left) and sat up to make her plans.

King Lucas thought he was getting rid of her by sending her to the Snoring Cave instead of with the soldiers, but if Theodore said there was such a thing as a giant, then she believed him. She would go to that cave and cut off a piece of the giant's hair, or mustache, or eyelash, or whatever she could get her hands on. That's what her father would do, she was sure of it.

She couldn't wait to see the king's face when he found out he really *had* been living on someone else's stomach all his life.

It took a lot of thinking before Persimmony finally knocked on the door to the room where Worvil was sleeping. There was no answer. She opened it quietly and called out, "Worvil! Worvil, wake up! I've got wonderful news to tell you!"

"Gowaymmmshleepinmmmmmmf," said a lump in the middle of the bed.

"Worvil, the king has chosen us to go to the Snoring Cave and find the giant!"

The lump jumped and tumbled to the ground tangled in blankets. "WHAT?"

"Everyone is so envious of us. I mean, who wouldn't want to explore a cave looking for a sleeping giant? It will be loads of fun."

Worvil untangled himself from the blankets and stuck his head out to stare at Persimmony. "But I don't want to go to the Western Shore! I don't like caves! I want to stay right here where there are no Leafeaters and no tortoises and no Rumblebumps and especially no giants!"

"Oh, don't be silly. We have the easiest job of all. We just have to go into the cave, peek to see if there's the head of a giant there, and then leave. Nothing to it."

"But the giant might wake up and eat us!"

"Giants don't eat worriers. They taste sour."

"But he might not know that until after he had bitten into me and spit me out again. I wonder what it's like to be eaten. Do you suppose that you'd actually *feel* the teeth breaking your bones, or would you have a heart attack and die of fright first?"

"Worvil, don't you see that if the giant does wake up, the most dangerous place to be in the entire kingdom is the castle? This whole mountain would collapse. Much better to be inside of a cave and out of harm's way, *I* think."

"Good point," said Worvil.

"Of course it is. And besides, there might not even be a giant."

"Oh, but there might be, there might be. And it's the *might be* that worries me."

"Listen," Persimmony said more gently, "I promise that I'll let you know if there's anything you need to worry about, and you promise me that you won't worry until I do. Okay?"

Worvil was quiet for a moment. "I have a feeling

I'm going to come back from this trip two inches shorter."

"What? Why would you be shorter?"

"I've been getting shorter for years. If you shrink from danger often enough, then you start to—well—shrink. Every month I have to roll up my sleeves and trouser legs a little more." He heaved a long and heavy sigh. "One of my cousins was brave once. He jumped into the ocean to save a little girl who was drowning."

"See? You have courage running through your blood after all."

"A shark got him."

Worvil was finally persuaded, however, and the two made their way to the great hall, where the king was having a special breakfast served to the two search parties. Theodore had not yet arrived. Persimmony wasn't very happy to be sitting next to the archaeologist Dustin Dexterhoof, who was a walking dust cloud, but at least she had Worvil to her right. The twelve soldiers bound for the Leafeater city were happily stuffing their faces with banana fritters. Captain Gidding, who Persimmony thought was much more heroic-looking now that he was awake, was absentmindedly stirring salt into his tea and smiling up at the ceiling as if he saw a magnificent sunrise behind the wooden beams there.

When all the guests had had their fill, Lucas rose to his feet solemnly, wiped mango juice from his chin with the back of his hand, and cleared his throat. "My faithful, unimpeachable, indefatigable subjects, some of you will depart today to face crafty, cowardly enemies hiding underground among the worms and scheming up their diabolical mashed potatoes . . ."

"*Machinations,* Your Highness," whispered Professor Quibble.

"Others of you will undertake an investigation of gargantuan importance, to prove—or disprove—the existence of that dangerous creature they call a . . ." He paused as he remembered that he had forbidden any mention of the giant and that the soldiers did not know about the rumors. "A cleft-lipped razor-barbed man-eating stingray," he finished.

"Persimmony," Worvil whispered, "I've changed my mind. I don't want to go after all."

"Shhhh! I can't hear the king," Persimmony whispered back.

Lucas adjusted his crown and smiled broadly at the faces of his guests. "Of course, I know why you are willing to risk your lives in such heroic tasks: Me. You love your king. If I may say so, I don't blame you—"

Lucas was interrupted by the sudden appearance of the potter, who was carrying a bulky sack over one shoulder. "So sorry, so sorry," he said, out of breath.

"You're late," snapped Lucas. "You missed breakfast and a very eloquent speech. I spent a whole hour looking up all the big words in the dictionary."

"Well, if the soldiers hadn't dumped all of my pots in a pile in the kitchen and the cook hadn't started putting them away with the royal dishes, I could have come a lot sooner. I have some gifts." He drew one clay pot out of his sack and set it in front of Worvil. He set a second one in front of Persimmony. With delight, she immediately recognized it as the elegant pot she had seen on the grass outside the potter's cottage. When he gave it to her, he looked her straight in the eye and whispered, *"Find the giant. Quickly. Everything will depend on you."* She looked back at him questioningly, but he said nothing more.

"She shouldn't get one!" said King Lucas. "Give the pot to Captain Gidding. He's in charge of the assault against the Leafeaters—he's important!"

"Oh, I don't mind." Captain Gidding smiled and went back to studying the ceiling again.

"The pot belongs to the one to whom I give it," said Theodore, "and I give this one to Persimmony."

Lucas was about to object again but stopped when the potter drew a third pot out of his sack and set it at the head of the table. It was a pot fit for a king—large, stout, and covered with intricate patterns traced in the clay. King Lucas gave a squeal of pleasure and thrust his hand deep into the pot. An instant later, he pulled it out again as if he had been stung. His hand was soaking wet. "What's this?" he cried, and licked his palm. "Milk! I hate milk! I wanted pepper, not milk. What is the meaning of this?"

"I only make the pots," said Theodore. "I am not responsible for what comes out of them."

Persimmony gazed at her pot with a bubble of excitement in her stomach. What could it hold? A long, shiny sword sharp enough to slice through the skull of a giant with a single blow? A suit of armor glimmering like the sun on the sea, so light that she could run a race in it, so strong that a whole army of Leafeaters could not penetrate it?

She put her hand in cautiously, wary of what had

happened to the king, but her fingers met something soft. When she pulled it out, she saw that it was a feather with a long, white plume.

The bubble in her stomach popped. Disappointed, she looked at the potter. "A feather, Theodore? Is that all? How is a feather going to help me?"

"I have no idea," said Theodore, inspecting the feather curiously. "But you will need it, that is certain."

Meanwhile Worvil was inspecting his own pot. It was very thin and very tall, just large enough for his hand to fit into, and though he tried several times to look he could not see what was inside. Reach into that? With who-knows-what-unseen-slimy-disgusting-creatures waiting at the bottom to bite off his fingers? But he did, though it cost him several heartbeats, and nothing bit him. He pulled out a long, round, hollow piece of wood. One end was flattened, and there were small holes, evenly spaced, down the length of the wood.

Guafnoggle took the strange object out of Worvil's hands, turned it over several times, put the flat end in his mouth, and blew hard. Out came a high-pitched, ear-piercing "SQUEEEEEEEEEEEEEAK!"

"I know what that is!" cried the archaeologist. "I once discovered one buried underneath a decayed fishing boat. Well, of course that one was a lot *dirtier* than this one—perhaps the objects are distant cousins rather than *exactly* the same thing—but to come to the point—"

"*What is it?*" asked Lucas, Persimmony, and Worvil at the same time.

"It's an ancient musical instrument called a *flute*!" said the archaeologist.

"That's not music," said Persimmony, holding her ears. "If anything will wake up the giant, *that* will."

"Shhhh!" said Lucas at the mention of the giant.

Professor Quibble tapped his chin thoughtfully. "So . . . the kingdom faces its worst crisis in history armed with a feather, a flute, and a pot of milk."

"We're doomed," Worvil groaned.

Captain Gidding rose from his seat. "Your Highness, I have just finished composing a poetic ode to sweet potatoes, in fifty-two stanzas. May I recite it for you?"

"No!" said Lucas, and that was the end of breakfast.

The two parties departed from the front gates soon afterward. Persimmony, Worvil, and Guafnoggle headed west. Captain Gidding and the twelve soldiers headed east.

Standing in the highest tower, King Lucas watched miserably as they departed. He had carried his pot up with him and every so often would peek inside, hoping that somehow there had been a mistake and the milk would magically turn into pepper—or at least something besides milk. Gold would do. But apparently the milk was there to stay.

"I'll punish that wicked potter. I'll force him to do nothing but make pots until he gives me pepper."

A cool breeze blew through the window. Lucas shivered and turned away. "I think I'll take a very long bubble bath. In fact, I think I could spend the rest of the week taking bubble baths." He started down the stairs, but something warm against his leg stopped him.

He looked down. It was a gray cat, its hair matted and its bones sticking out sharply from its thin body. Lucas gave it a kick, and the cat let out a cry of pain. "Get out of my way, you ugly beast," he muttered, and took another step down the stairs. Then an idea occurred to him, and he turned around and came back. He took a bowl, set it down on the floor, and poured the entire contents of Theodore's pot into it.

"Ha! If that potter thinks I'm going to drink

his milk, he can think again. There it goes, every drop, down the belly of a mangy animal. Serves him right!"

And with that King Lucas stomped down the tower steps, leaving behind an overjoyed cat lapping up the milk as fast as its little tongue could go.

Chapter 12

In Which Persimmony Meets a Very Important Person

*B*rave *of heart and* light of foot, the heroes ran over the western rocks with no thought but to find the giant. Nothing could stop them.

Well, perhaps that was wrong. After all, if nothing could stop a hero, Persimmony thought, the story would be a boring one. *Nothing could stop them—except, perhaps, a tidal wave.* Yes, that was better. A tidal wave on a rocky shore was just the thing. A small one, at least. She would cling to a rock valiantly, with Worvil holding on to her legs and Guafnoggle paddling with his big feet until the wave had passed, washing away the large clump of seaweed that had been hiding the very cave they had come to seek.

So far, however, the story was not going as she had imagined it. Instead of traveling on foot like any sensible person would, Guafnoggle had insisted on *rolling* down Mount Majestic. He grasped hold of his toes, and Worvil—carried inside the circle of the Rumblebump's arms and feet—went spinning downhill like an animal caught in a rolling barrel. Persimmony ran as fast as she could to keep up. When the Rumblebump suddenly came to a stop, Worvil was catapulted through the air.

"OUCH!" Worvil gingerly rubbed the swelling lump where his head had struck a rock.

Guafnoggle, lying spread-eagled on the stone-riddled ground, laughed. "You shouldn't have let go! I told you not to let go, so you shouldn't have done it!"

"Oh, my head! I'll never count to ten again, thanks to you!" Worvil stood up dizzily and tried practicing on his fingers. Persimmony, arriving breathless a few minutes afterward, fell into a heap beside him and gazed out at the scene before her. They had stopped at the edge of the grassy headlands at the westernmost end of Mount Majestic. In fact, if Guafnoggle and Worvil had rolled a few feet farther they would have rolled right off the edge of a sharp cliff.

As she climbed down the rocky slopes, Persimmony wished she had huge, leathery, flexible feet like Guafnoggle, who skipped easily over the surfaces and jagged edges. Her own bare feet felt every sharp point. "Guafnoggle!" she yelled above the roar of the surf. "Wait for us!" Below them, the sea lay like a great shining mirror, and Guafnoggle ran eagerly over the rocks to find himself in it. Behind them rose the stony western face of Mount Majestic. Along its rough surface were dozens of caves, some merely cracks, others gaping mouths.

One cave would lead to a giant's head.

"Well," she sighed, "if Guafnoggle deserts us, I guess we can go listen by each cave until we hear one that snores."

"I just remembered that I'm allergic to caves," said Worvil, shivering.

"That's impossible. No one is allergic to caves."

"Bats. Every time I see one, I sneeze."

"When have you ever seen a bat?"

"My grandmother once told me a story about bats. I sneezed the rest of the night."

She gripped a moss-covered rock and lowered herself down to another rock before she answered: "Isn't there a single tiny part of you—anywhere at all—that is a little bit excited that you might get to see something no one else believes is there? That you've been chosen to do a task no one thinks you can do, and you have a chance to prove that you can?"

Worvil looked down at his feet, rubbed his chest, and patted his bald head. "No, I don't think so. I was chosen once to carry a pail of water for my father. I dropped it and broke my toe. I don't like being chosen. Oh, I should have never left the castle! I should have chained myself to the bedpost, or dressed as a kitchen servant and spent the rest of my life peeling potatoes. But no." He covered his face in one hand. "It would be no use. Because what if there really is a giant? What if he wakes up? Can you imagine, Persimmony? When he stood up, all of the earth and the stones on top of him would fall like rain onto the fields and the orchards and the beaches. Who could survive that? Farmers would be buried under the flying ruins of a falling mountain. The fishermen would hide in their boats, but what good are boats against a creature so big? And *after* he was awake! There would be no escaping from him. The trees would be like shrubs to him, and the houses like tiny mounds of dirt under his feet. And the people would be so little he would hardly notice if he walked right on top of them—he might even get down on his hands and knees and pick them up one by one, because after all he would be so *hungry* after sleeping underground for—"

Worvil's right foot slipped and he tumbled forward, grasping in vain for a place to catch himself. Persimmony saw his little body roll over a protruding ledge and disappear. A scream ripped through the wind.

"WORVIL!" she cried in horror. She quickly and carefully crawled toward the ledge where he had fallen and looked over it, terrified of what she would see.

Worvil's rolled-up trouser leg had caught on a sharp rock jutting out from the ledge. He was dangling upside down, his head floating only about six inches above a large, flat stone surface. The many folds of his clothing hung like a sack over his head, and he was blindly shrieking as he imagined himself falling to his doom.

Guafnoggle, who had heard the screaming and started bounding back up the slopes, took one look and burst into a fit of laughter. Persimmony had to laugh in spite of herself. Climbing over the ledge, she wrapped her arms around Worvil's waist and lifted him up enough to loosen the trouser leg from the rock—surprised at how little he weighed. Then she lowered him till he lay on the flat surface. He stopped screaming and looked around, dazed. When he realized he was safe, he flung his arms around Persimmony's neck.

"You saved me!" he said joyfully. "I owe my life to you!"

Persimmony had always dreamed of someone saying that to her, but she wanted to actually deserve it when those words came. "Well," she admitted, trying gently to loosen his fingers from around her throat so she could breathe, "it was really your trousers that saved you."

"But you caught me! I would have plunged ten thousand feet into the sea."

"You would have fallen about six inches."

"I would have died!"

"You would have gotten another bump on your head."

But Worvil heard nothing. "How can I ever repay you?" he asked, staring solemnly into her eyes.

Persimmony had to work hard not to laugh again. "I'll try to think of something," she said as seriously as she could. Then she saw that Guafnoggle was waving to them, and that he was carrying a torch. She helped Worvil to his feet, locked arms with him to keep him from falling again, and slowly followed the Rumblebump.

Guafnoggle led them past many large open-mouthed caves to a small one that was almost hidden underneath a large, protruding rock. Its opening was low and wide. Sure enough, as the little group drew close they could hear a SOUND coming from deep within the earth.

Persimmony grabbed the torch from Guafnoggle's hand. She didn't like the thought of tiptoeing up to a sleeping giant with one companion whose big feet pounded the stone floor like a drum and another who was likely to scream in terror at any moment. "I'll go in alone," she announced. "Worvil, you can stay out here and stand guard with Guafnoggle." Persimmony spotted an empty oyster shell and put it in the pocket of her dress. It was as sharp as a razor—perfect for cutting off a lock of hair.

She flashed a wide smile to show she was not afraid, then turned toward the blackness and crawled inside.

And the truth was, she felt no fear—yet. In fact, she was almost disappointed by her own calmness. Even the most courageous hero should be a little scared in the face of enormous danger. Every so often Persimmony stopped walking and jumped up and down a bit to try to get some butterflies moving in her stomach, but instead of fluttering they seemed to be huddling together into a tighter and tighter ball.

The cave was dark and cold and wet and endless. The damp chill seeped into her bones. The torch in her hand rattled and cast an eerie path of light against the cave walls around her. The roar of the waves on the shore grew fainter and fainter, but the SOUND continued—deeper than any voice she had ever heard, louder and longer than the growl of any beast.

There was not just the SOUND to deal with. There was the suction. Persimmony felt pulled forward with every step. At first she thought a strong wind behind her was causing this strange sensation, but as she got farther away from the cave's entrance she realized that this force was coming from *within* the mountain. It was sucking her in . . .

Toward what?

Step by step she continued on, and with each step the world she knew grew more and more distant. Far behind her, Worvil was probably biting his nails anxiously waiting for her to return. Far above her, the king was probably sitting on his throne listening to the professor drone on about multiplication tables. Her mother and Prunella were probably sitting cross-legged on the floor of their cottage weaving willow wands into baskets as they did every morning. Farmers were plowing their fields, shopkeepers were counting money, and coconut pickers were climbing palm trees. But here on this stone road into the heart of the mountain there was only a young girl with bare feet and nothing to hold on to but a torch and no sound but the SOUND, wrapping itself around her, pulling her closer. And with each step a little piece of her bravery fell off and rolled away.

She stopped once to catch her breath and looked down to find that she had tied the hem of her dress into a dozen knots without even realizing it. And then something strange started to happen to her feet. They decided they weren't going to do a thing she wanted them to do. *Keep walking,* she told them angrily. But for every five steps forward, they took a step backward, and rubbed their cold toes against each other, and stuck stubbornly to the cold stone floor.

Persimmony was concentrating so much on putting one foot in front of the other that she didn't even notice that the walls on either side of her were growing farther and farther apart. All at once she became aware that she was no longer walking on stone but on something soft and cushiony, like a carpet. She knelt down and reached out her hand.

Hair. There was no doubt about it. Piles and piles of it, like great coils of rope, or like mounds of fishing nets along a pier.

It was only then that Persimmony knew that she was not in a narrow tunnel anymore but in an enormous space, and that she was not the only one there. Trembling so much that she could hardly hold the torch, she lifted the light higher . . . and higher . . . and higher . . .

Her legs gave way beneath her, and she sank to her knees. She had not imagined big enough. She had only thought about *finding* the giant. She hadn't thought about *seeing* it. She had believed in it, but she hadn't really considered it being real. She had not stopped to picture in her mind what it would be like to be here, alone, looking at it—him.

There weren't enough words to describe him. There weren't enough words to *think* him. How many different ways can you say "big"? Huge. Enormous. Gigantic. Immense. Colossal. Towering. Mighty. Majestic.

Giant.

The waves of gray hair under her feet poured out of a huge forehead above her. Deep wrinkles stretched far into the darkness. There was an eyelid—closed, oh, what a relief!—and another eyelid, and eyelashes sweeping onto a wrinkled cheek, pitted and creased with age. Could that tower rising high above possibly be a nose? The nostrils twitched with the force

of a tremendous breath. And then she saw—nestled within another forest of gray hair, farther ahead, disappearing into the dark of the endless cave—a mouth, a shuddering lip, the white glimmer of teeth.

She couldn't see the whole face at once—she had to move her torch so that its light fell in patches on the rough, pale skin. Could all of those patches of face in the light belong to the same face? It was so strange and marvelous that she had an impulse to reach out and stroke the giant's leathery cheek to see if it was real.

The giant lay with his head turned slightly toward the tunnel from which Persimmony had come. The stone ledge above him had once shielded him from the glare of the sun when he had first settled down for his nap. Now it shielded him from the earth that covered him with its thick blanket. The tunnel had brought breezes from the sea to cool the giant's face. Now it carried his breath and the sound of his snoring—a long, deep, rattling snore as the giant breathed in and breathed in and breathed in. What would it sound like when he began to breathe out, Persimmony wondered? He must have been sleeping peacefully for such a long, long time to be breathing so slowly and so deeply. And so he would sleep for another thousand years, or awaken at any moment and open his eyes and see—

Fear coiled itself around her heart. This was the Person whose feet the Leafeaters were blindly digging toward, the giant feet that would trample everyone as if this were a kingdom of ants. The king didn't believe it. Captain Gidding and the soldiers didn't know about the giant as they went off to wage war. The people of the island had not been warned.

Find the giant, Theodore had whispered to her at breakfast. *Quickly. Everything will depend on you.* Everything would depend on her? That was too much to carry. What if she failed? What if—?

Persimmony buried her head in the folds of her dress and gripped the hairy carpet underneath her to keep herself from floating away. And then one of her hands touched something familiar.

Bringing the torch closer, she saw that it was a basket. And not just any basket—the slender willow branches were braided together just as she had done so many times, and Prunella had done, and her mother had done. This was a Smudge basket. But she knew her mother had never seen the giant. Her mother couldn't keep a secret that big. Inside were two small, brown lumps. She picked them up. They were made of pine needles, woven and knotted together carefully into two shapes. One was unmistakably a turtle. The other— what was the other? She couldn't quite make it out.

He made little animals out of twigs and pine nee-dles, Prunella had said. *He made me a turtle once. I don't know where it went.*

No, it couldn't be.

Had *he* been here? Had he knelt where she was kneeling, and looked up at that same giant face, and felt this same knot of fear inside? What had he done? Had he run out again, dropping the basket in his hurry? Did he tell anyone? Or had he— She caught her breath and looked at the teeth in the distant shadows. No, it was too horrible to think of. She pushed it out of her mind.

But she felt a little less alone. Carefully she wedged the torch between two rocks and took the oyster shell out of her pocket. Her hands shook as she lifted a lock of the giant's hair and rubbed the sharp edge of the shell against it, quietly, firmly, breaking one strand and then another. Just as she cut through the last strand, the Snore suddenly erupted into a sput-tering Snort, and Persimmony was so startled that she dropped the shell and nearly screamed. The giant's nose wrinkled and his head shifted slightly— though *slightly* for him was like an earthquake around Persimmony. She felt the coils of hair buckle under her knees, and though the giant's eyes were closed, she could see his great gray-bearded mouth moving, forming silent words. Finally, the giant sank back into his dream and was still.

Persimmony breathed and waited until her frozen fingers had the strength to move again. Then she tied the lock of hair around her waist like a belt. This was her proof.

Picking up the torch and the basket, and taking one last look at the giant's closed eyes, she turned and quietly ran back toward the tunnel.

When she emerged from the cave into the sunlight again, she felt as if she were waking from a dream.

"Persimmony!" Worvil cried, flinging his stubby arms around her waist while Guafnoggle turned somersaults of joy beside him. "Oh, Persimmony, I thought I'd never see you again! I thought you'd been eaten by bats, or fallen into a bottomless pit, or—" He stopped and backed away slightly, staring at the belt of hair his hands had touched.

Persimmony looked at the squashed little potato-faced man with his hands stuffed into his rolled-up sleeves. His forehead was stamped with the footprints of a hundred worries, and his wide eyes swam in memories of birthday candles and bee stings and falling turtles.

"Seaweed," she said, smiling in what she hoped

was a convincing way. Her heart was thumping in her chest so loudly that she was afraid Worvil would hear it. "I got cold, so I wrapped it around me." Guafnoggle looked doubtfully at her. If anyone knew seaweed, it was a Rumblebump. "There's no giant," she continued, trying to laugh carelessly, but the laugh came out as more like a hiccup. "The snoring sound is just wind blowing through a hole higher up the mountain. It's just like the professor said: There's a logical explanation for everything."

Worvil stared at her for a long moment. She knew he didn't believe her, though he wanted to desperately. "Okay, that's not *exactly* true," she admitted.

"Oh, I knew it, I knew it," Worvil wailed, putting his hands to his head as if tear out his hair—if he had any hair to tear. "There *is* a giant under the mountain!" Guafnoggle had the sense to stuff his coat in his mouth to contain his glee.

"Not a big one," Persimmony said quickly. "Actually quite a tiny giant, so small I could hardly see it."

"A *tiny* giant?"

"Big, small, what's the difference? I mean, why is a person's size important anyway? After all, look at you—most people may think you're short, but *I* know that inside of that shrinking body there's a giant waiting to burst out."

"There is?" he said in a small voice.

"Of course! Why else would I trust you to guard the cave while I'm gone?"

"While you're ... gone?" he said in an even smaller voice.

"You asked how you could repay me for saving your life. Well, here is how. I'll go back and tell the king what I saw, just as he asked me to do, and you stay here and keep watch so that no one else can go inside and wake the giant up. Guafnoggle will protect you. And remember, you promised not to worry until I did. Do I look worried to you?" She regretted ever trying to wake up the butterflies in her stomach, since they were now coming in swarms. "Don't worry," she told Worvil, taking his oversized sleeves in her hands and trying hard to look cheerful and deadly serious at the same time, "but guard it with your life." She added, "You're bigger than you think you are."

Then she turned to the Rumblebump. "Guafnoggle, can you remember anyone else ever going into this cave?"

Guafnoggle's brow wrinkled, and he twisted a lock of hair several times around his nose to think. Then his eyes lit up. "The Grandest Grand Stomper of All! Yes, yes, I remember! We called him that because he once saved twelve starfish from being eaten by a very hungry sea otter, which is more than any other Grand Stomper had ever saved, and he was our Grand Stomper for months and months and was the very best saver, until he went away for a long time, but then he came back and we laughed and waved to him as he went into the Snoring Cave, but that was many years ago, and come to think of it, he looked a lot like you — same color hair, same eyes, same nose, same mouth, same — "

He *had* been here! The mad swarm of butterflies in her stomach began to dance. *He looked like me!* Her numb fingers and toes tingled with a new warm glow. And suddenly, against all reason, she wanted to run back into the cave again. She had the strange feeling that this time it would be her father lying there asleep, and not a giant. His was the face she longed to see.

"But" — she wasn't sure she wanted to know the answer — "did you see him come *out* of the Snoring Cave again?"

"Don't know. We all decided to go swimming, and I was the very best swimmer then, and I still am, and I was teaching everyone else how to ride a wave backward and forgot all about him. But why wouldn't he come out again? Everyone who goes into a cave comes out again, unless you fall asleep, which I did once, because I was very full from eating so many seaweed sandwiches for supper, and it was hours and hours before I . . ."

Persimmony didn't wait for Guafnoggle's cyclone of words to end. She bounded up the rocks toward the cliff face. But when she was out of their sight, she turned to the right and began heading south, around the mountain instead of up. There was no time to waste. She was the daughter of Simeon Smudge, Discoverer of Giants, and she had a job to do now. She was going straight to the Willow Woods to find the soldiers.

◖◐ Chapter 13 ◑◗

In Which Persimmony Drives a Hard Bargain and Worvil Catches a Star in His Pocket

$\mathcal{M}$ount Majestic! Persimmony *had* seen it in the distance every single day of her life—like a huge, watchful guardian. Trees would some-day fall, the waves would wash away the sand, but Mount Majestic would always be standing solid and dependable—rising or falling, but *there.*

At least, that's what she had always believed.

Now the flags atop the castle seemed to shiver and nod and whisper to each other in the wind. And so they should, for they were flying above a great and terrible secret.

Before long she had left the western rocks behind

her and had come to a road leading east through the small village of Bristlebend. She could smell the fresh bread baking and hear the mooing of a cow as its owner milked it—as if this were just an ordinary morning. As if the sun were shining on an island with nothing to hide and nothing to fear. But Persimmony felt as if someone had turned her upside down and started shaking her, till her head was a jumble and the earth was falling into the sky.

"You look like a young lady who knows the value of a good colander. You never know when you're going to need to rinse your spinach." A peddler stood before her, smiling broadly and holding a large round bowl with holes in the bottom for washing vegetables. He wore four hats stacked on his head and a belt with pouches in which were stuffed dozens of bottles of varying shapes and sizes, holding mysterious liquids. Beside him stood a donkey that was carrying the rest of the merchandise in two enormous bundles on either side of its back.

Persimmony couldn't hold in the news a moment longer. "There's a giant sleeping under Mount Majestic, and the Leafeaters are digging toward his feet, and if the giant wakes up we're all going to die," she said in a rush.

"Now how about that!" said the peddler. "A giant,

you say? Very exciting indeed. In that case"—he flipped the colander upside down—"perhaps I could interest you in a Super-Deluxe Extra-Resistant Giant-Proof Helmet? Whatever the problem, Jim-Jo Pumpernickel has the cure!"

"You don't believe me!"

"Why shouldn't I believe you? I have no reason to think you are a liar." He put a hand on her shoulder. "My dear, you are obviously in a great hurry to tell people about this giant. You *could* waste time in this little village trying to interest people who are only concerned about baking bread and milking cows. But you look like a smart girl, and my guess is that you're heading east to Candlenut, which is known for being full of gossips. Drop a piece of news in Candlenut, and the entire island will know the next day. Therefore you should have said, 'There's a giant under Mount Majestic, and if you'll take me to Candlenut on your donkey so that I can tell people about it, I will make it worth your while.' A friendly wink wouldn't hurt either."

Persimmony thought hard for a moment. "Could you take me to the Willow Woods on your donkey?"

"Ha-ha! A girl after my own heart, always looking for a better bargain. But no, I have no business with the poison-tongued jumping tortoises today. I have a feeling they would prefer the blood in my veins to the merchandise in my pocket. Candlenut is near the border of the woods, and that's as far as I'll take you. For a price, of course. For example, that fascinating belt around your waist could make me a fortune at the wigmaker's."

"I can't give you this," Persimmony said, clutching it protectively. "This is the hair of the giant, and I need it to prove that he exists. But . . ." She had nothing of value to offer him. Her pockets held only a spool of thread, a few stones, and the feather Theodore had given her. She wouldn't give up the basket or its contents for the world. She thought quickly and swallowed hard. In desperate times, sacrifices were necessary. "But I do have a hat. It's a very nice hat—blue, with embroidered fruit on it. It looks a little like a drowning apple tree."

"A drowning apple tree hat would be a fair trade for taking you to Candlenut. But forgive me for saying that I can't seem to find it on your head."

"I don't exactly have it with me at the moment." But perhaps—after this crisis had ended—if it ended well—she could return to the woods and look for it. And if it didn't end well . . . "If you can get me to Candlenut as soon as possible, I promise that I'll do everything in my power to find you again and bring you the hat."

The peddler looked shrewdly at her and her belt of giant's hair through two pairs of eyeglasses. "Very well, then, I will take you on credit. This is not normally good business sense, since you could be bluffing and I may never see you or the afore-mentioned hat again. However, since the monetary benefits of being with you when you break the news of the giant to the generous citizens of Candlenut far outweigh the risk of giving you a free ride on my donkey—yes, I will take you. Up you go!" Before she could answer, he had swept her up and set her on the donkey's back between the two bundles, then climbed behind her and settled into his seat with a happy sigh. "Yes, yes, this is going to be very good for business. Onward, Toddle!"

And the poor overburdened donkey, evidently knowing that the benefits of obeying her master far outweighed the risk of a bruised rear end, used good business sense and trotted as quickly as her wobbly legs would carry her on the dusty road toward the green and gold blanket of farmlands beyond the village.

After Persimmony left, Worvil spent an entire hour with his eyes squeezed shut, hoping that he would

wake up from this nightmare and be safe at home. But then he wondered where home was anymore. Not his house that the mangrove tree had run off with, not the potter's cottage under the willow tree with a tortoise that might return, and certainly not the castle.

He was deep in the middle of pondering this dilemma when suddenly Guafnoggle jumped up and took off running across the rocks toward the sea.

"Wait! WAIT!" cried Worvil, terrified of being left alone with a cave that snored. He scrambled over a boulder and splashed into what he thought was a shallow tide pool between two rocks. After two steps he found himself up to his neck in sea water. A crab scuttled over his foot, and a school of fish swam into one shirt sleeve and out the other. Worvil screamed for help. There was no answer. Holding on to a clump of seaweed wedged between the rocks, he managed to pull himself out of the pool.

Where was Guafnoggle? Worvil remembered the potter's gift and felt in his pocket for the flute. It felt so powerless in his hands. He put his mouth on the narrow end, took a deep breath, and blew as hard as he could.

SQUAAAAAAWWWWK!!!!!

He jumped at the noise and thrust the flute as

quickly as he could back into his pocket, vowing never to take it out again until this whole fiasco was over.

The roar of the surf grew louder, and he was hit by a wall of white foam.

"I'm wet!" he said aloud. "What if I come down with pneumonia?" For the next few minutes he forgot about the Snoring Cave and began looking for a sheltered place away from the breaking waves. He made his way over the slippery stones toward a little cove he had spotted on his way down. The surface of the water there was almost entirely hidden by huge, tangled clumps of seaweed—a blanket of reds and greenish browns that gently swelled with the current. Worvil found a flat rock in the sun and sat down to dry off and to worry.

No sooner had he done so than the entire blanket of seaweed erupted and came splashing out of the water toward him. Worvil let out a shriek, then he recognized one particular clump as the long, wet hair of Guafnoggle. Dripping and giggling, a wave of Rumblebumps rose out of the water and poured onto the rocky shore, leaving wet footprints and trailing long, tangled locks of hair that Worvil had mistaken for seaweed.

"Did we fool you?" cried Guafnoggle in delight at

Worvil's startled face. But he didn't stop to talk, for the Rumblebumps were already racing off to their next game.

The Rumblebumps were no bigger than Worvil himself (though their feet were so large that if they stood on their tiptoes they would be the tallest people in the kingdom). With all of their layers and layers of shirts and coats and vests and dresses, covered with pockets of all shapes and sizes, they had that lumpy-potato look that Worvil had in his too-big trousers and rolled-up sleeves. But there the similarities ended. The Rumblebumps' round faces (slightly bluish from spending so much time in the water) were shining with excitement and curiosity, and their seaweed-hair billowed around them like wings as it dried in the sun. Worvil almost believed they would start flying at any moment. They ran from one tide pool to another—anywhere the waves had touched and left water to linger among the rocks—scooping their hands into each one and letting loose great peals of laughter.

One elderly Rumblebump whom the others called Barnacle hobbled by Worvil with his many pockets bulging and squirming. He reached into them one at a time and took out a jellyfish, a sea urchin, two fiddler crabs, clams, mussels, scallops, and a handful of tiny silver tuna, and laid them gently in the water to be washed out to sea again by the tide.

"What are you doing?" Worvil asked.

"Saving them, of course! Are you blind as a bat that you cannot see all the creatures left to die on the shore? We are the savers, and if we did not save them, what on earth would we use all our pockets for?"

And then Barnacle was off again to fill his pockets with more sea creatures in need of rescue.

"I've found a horseshoe crab!" came an excited voice from the throng.

"Here's a snail!" squealed another.

But Worvil was more interested in finding Guafnoggle than in paying much attention to what the rest of the Rumblebumps were doing. He finally spotted him leaning over a shallow pool trying to catch a very nervous seahorse.

"Please," Worvil said timidly, "couldn't we go back to the Snoring Cave now?"

"Shhhh!" whispered Guafnoggle. "What did you do that for? You just scared him off again!"

"Persimmony said not to leave it. She told us to guard it with our lives, and—why are you looking at me like that?"

Guafnoggle was staring at him with his eyes wide open and his mouth agape. "You found it."

"Found what?"

But Guafnoggle had already leaped to the top of one of the boulders and was yelling as loudly as he could, "He found it, he found it, he's been chosen, come quickly, come and see!"

The Rumblebumps came running to where Worvil stood and gathered around him with a kind of quiet, reverent delight.

A young Rumblebump girl, whose hair was wrapped around her head in a crown of red braids, touched his arm softly. "You've been chosen," she whispered.

Worvil's nose trembled. "Chosen for what? Why is everyone looking at me? What did I do?"

Guafnoggle pointed solemnly (as solemnly as possible for a Rumblebump, anyway) toward Worvil's right foot. Worvil looked down. Tucked in the rolled-up cuff of his trouser leg was a small orange starfish, hardly bigger than the palm of his hand. "A starfish is rare and precious and the most beautiful thing there is, and anyone who saves a starfish is the new Grand Stomper of the Rumblebumps—that means you."

"No, no, no! I didn't save the starfish! I just acci-

dentally fell into a tide pool and the starfish must have gotten stuck inside my cuff. Here—you can have it!" Worvil picked up the starfish and pushed it into Guafnoggle's hands.

Guafnoggle burst out laughing and handed it back. "No, silly, the starfish chose you, not me!"

"But I can't possibly be the Grand Stomper of the Rumblebumps!"

"Why not?"

It was so obvious why not that Worvil couldn't think of a single thing to say. He grasped for a practical reason. "Because—because I've got to guard the Snoring Cave, remember?"

"What's in the Snoring Cave?" asked the red-braided girl eagerly.

Guafnoggle was very famous among the Rumble-bumps because of the vast amount of knowledge he had picked up while working at the castle, and he was not about to miss this opportunity to show some of it off. "Oh, Sallyroo, you will never guess if you guessed as many times as there are fish in the sea," he said, doing a somersault. A button popped off his coat. "The archaeologist lost his belt buckle and had to dig up the whole dungeon to find it again, and since the king is the center of the world he is tied to the sun by an invisible string and so he had to get the potter to come and pour milk on the pancakes, but then the Leafeaters starting tickling the historian's feet, so he hid in the Snoring Cave, and if one plus one equals three and there is no proof to the contrary, then there is a giant taking a nap under Mount Majestic!"

"That wasn't right at all!" protested Worvil. "Well, the last part was right—about there being a giant asleep under the mountain, but—"

He couldn't finish because all the Rumblebumps suddenly burst out laughing—not in a mocking way like the professor and the king, but as if someone had told them the most marvelous story they had ever heard.

"We must wake him up!" said one. "What fun it would be. He must know some awfully big games."

"NO!" cried Worvil. "That's exactly what we *can't* do. Don't you see that the mountain might break into a thousand pieces and the castle might be destroyed and rocks might start falling all around us and—oh! What if we were trapped underneath the rocks? What if we didn't have any homes anymore?"

"Then we would find new caves and build new houses."

"But the giant would have very big feet!" said Worvil.

"So do we!" said Barnacle, proudly shaking one of his own. "Are you dumb as driftwood to be scared of someone just because his toes are larger than yours?"

"But he might have such big feet and stomp so hard that the island itself would crumble and fall into the sea, and everyone would be drifting out in the middle of the ocean!"

"Then the giant could save us. He could—" Sallyroo's eyes lit up as the idea came to her: "He could put us in *his* pockets!"

The thought of riding in a giant's pockets was so exciting to the Rumblebumps that for a few moments Worvil could hardly get a word in edgewise. Everyone was talking at once about how many of them might fit into one pocket, and who would stand on whose shoulders so that the Rumblebump on top could peek out of the pocket and see what was going on and describe it to the rest.

"There would be nothing fun about it," Worvil pleaded, wishing for the hundredth time that Persimmony had stayed with him. "There is so much to worry about, and—where are you going?" But he knew immediately where they were going. The Rumblebumps were bouncing merrily over the rocks toward the Snoring Cave to wake up the giant and ride in his pockets.

"Stop, stop!" he yelled desperately. "Your Grand Stomper says stop!"

And to his great surprise, the Rumblebumps did stop. They turned to look at him, disappointed but respectful.

Worvil stood still, his mind whirling. What had he just done? From what deep down, secret, rash, foolishly daring part of him had that outburst come? It was too late now to take it back. "I—I—" he stammered, and said apologetically: "I forbid you to wake up the giant."

Sallyroo climbed over the rocks and clasped his hand. "So you will be our Grand Stomper?"

In his mind Worvil saw the giant, the *real* Grand Stomper, grand and enormous and towering over the world, stomping the island into mango pulp. He closed his eyes and nodded.

Guafnoggle yelled, "Hail, Worvil!" and the Rumblebumps echoed, "Hail, hail!" Before he had time to protest, Worvil was being hoisted onto someone's shoulders and paraded down the shore.

"To the Meeting Cave! Prepare the feasts, the games, the dancing . . ."

"Oh, be careful," said Worvil, "you might drop me on my head!" But his words were lost in the crash of the waves and the cheers of his new followers.

Chapter 14

In Which It Pays to Be Polite, but Grammar Can Get Sticky

*B*y *the time* Persimmony, Jim-Jo Pumpernickel the peddler, and Toddle the donkey arrived in Candlenut, Persimmony's stomach had forgotten it had ever had breakfast, and her bottom was so sore from the donkey's back that she wondered if she would ever walk again. But her hunger and soreness were nothing compared to the sight that greeted them when they stopped in the main square.

Two Leafeaters were sitting in a pile of toppled egg crates. Egg yolks dribbled down their pale faces and made yellow puddles in their laps. Egg shells covered their eyes. Their legs were stuck in fallen crates as if they were wearing big gooey shoes. Above them stood a very angry spice merchant with his hands on his hips and an even angrier dairy farmer who owned the eggs.

"And *that* is what you get for insulting me!" yelled the merchant.

"My dear sir," said one of the Leafeaters, who was gripping a handful of paintbrushes in one hand and wiping egg yolk off his nose with the other, "no insult was intended. You said, 'The pepper barrels are empty, I'm afraid, but once you and your friend smells oregano, you'll never want pepper again.' I simply corrected your mistake: It should be 'you and your friend *smell*.'"

"There you go again! I'll have you know that I and all my friends bathe with soap and water every morning."

"I was merely pointing out the lack of agreement."

"What, you don't agree that the pepper barrels are empty? Go and see for yourself! Any new pepper must go straight to the king."

"No, I meant that if you want your sentence to be grammatically correct, your verb, *smell*, must agree with your subject, *you and your friend*."

"My subject? Only the king has subjects. I'm a loyal citizen, do you hear me? How dare you call me a traitor?"

By now a large crowd had gathered in the square, and though most of the people there had little love for the king, they were all ready to defend their neighbor's loyalty when a *Leafeater* had questioned it.

"This looks promising," whispered Jim-Jo Pumpernickel in Persimmony's ear. "Where there are broken eggs, there is a need for the very latest and best cleaning supplies. And where there is a crowd, there are many ears to hear important pieces of news. We will await our moment."

Persimmony stared at the Leafeaters. She knew where she had heard those voices before: in the Willow Woods at midnight.

The older of the two (judging from the wrinkles lining his pale face) sat up and glared at the spice merchant. "Did you say the king has used up *all the pepper in the kingdom*? For himself? Now that is the last straw. Year after year we have endured the selfishness and rudeness of those aboveground. You cut down our trees. You eat all the pepper—"

The younger Leafeater put a sticky hand on the other's shoulder. "Now Uncle, let's be fair. It's not their fault the king took all the pepper."

"I've lost three thimbles in the last month," said an old seamstress who owned a dress shop on the edge of town, "and I have no doubt in my mind that it was a Leafeater that hid them!"

"And everyone knows that if a person ventures too far into the woods he'll be kidnapped and taken underground forever to be used for your evil rituals!" said a sweet potato farmer (the farmer was not sweet, just his potatoes).

Persimmony felt her stomach tighten. What evil rituals might her father be undergoing at this moment? Did he somehow know, even seven years ago, that the Leafeaters would someday dig too close to the giant's feet? Did he try to warn them, and did they refuse to listen, kidnapping him instead?

"And you also climbed through my window and stole my rooster last year!" yelled a barefoot man wearing his nightshirt.

"I beg your pardon, we did nothing of the sort," the older Leafeater retorted.

"Well, one of your kind sure did. You all look alike."

"I am Rhedgrave Rhinkle," the Leafeater said severely, "and this is my nephew Rheuben Rhinkle, and for your information, sir, we both possess very distinctive Rhinkle family traits, including a noble upturn of our noses, larger than normal ears, and impeccably straight teeth. The Rhinkles also, unfortunately, have a tendency toward rheumatism, which would have made it quite impossible for me to climb through your window. Nor would any other Leafeater have done so, since our Code of Courtesy absolutely forbids stealing roosters, not to mention kidnapping and hiding thimbles from elderly women."

No kidnapping? Was he telling the truth? The knot in Persimmony's stomach loosened and fluttered in confusion.

"That will be for a jury to decide," said the Candlenut town magistrate, coming forward with a cold smile. "But there is one crime you are certainly guilty of, and that is *disturbing the peace.* You are under arrest."

"I think," said Rheuben quickly, "that if we could all sit down together and have a nice cup of tea with maple syrup, admire the weather, and speak politely, we would find that there is really nothing to argue about."

"Ha!" said the magistrate. "Mount Majestic itself will fall into the sea before I sit and have a friendly drink with a Leafeater!"

The other townspeople burst into laughter at the absurdity of both of these ideas.

"That's our moment," whispered the peddler, and he moved into the center of the crowd, tugging Persimmony behind him. "You laugh, ladies and gentlemen. But what if I were to tell you that even now the very foundations of that mountain might be shaking? Tell them, Persimmony." He shoved her forward.

Persimmony suddenly found herself facing a hundred pairs of suspicious eyes. She had been coming to this town for her entire life, and no one had ever taken any notice of her except to ask how much a basket cost or to tell her to keep her dirty hands off their best tomatoes. She took a deep breath. "There's a giant under Mount Majestic. I saw his head in a cave on the Western Shore with my own eyes, and we need to be prepared to—"

"Wh-wh-what did you say?" said a flower seller, clutching a handful of daisies and trying to faint.

"She said there's a giant under Mount Majestic," Jim-Jo said proudly. "Yes, folks, a giant—an enormous creature as big as the entire mountain, with teeth as big as a house and eyes like full moons and fire pouring out of its nostrils . . ."

"There wasn't any fire—" Persimmony started to object, but Jim-Jo kept right on going.

"But with a few of Jim-Jo Pumpernickel's Super-Deluxe Extra-Resistant Giant-Proof Helmets, you and your family will be as safe and snug as a pearl in an oyster. Do I have any buyers?"

People began snickering and nudging each other. Some rolled their eyes and walked off to continue their shopping. Persimmony felt her face growing hot. "Look, here's his hair!" she said, untying the makeshift belt and holding it up above her head. "I cut it off myself in the cave. I'm telling the truth! We really are in danger, and everyone needs to find a safe place to hide until—"

"Nonsense," said the sweet potato farmer. "That's like saying the sky isn't blue and the sun doesn't rise in the mornings. Wheat grows on cornstalks and tomatoes on apple trees. If you can't depend on Mount Majestic, what on earth can you depend on?"

"It isn't nonsense!" Persimmony cried.

"Wait a minute," said a woman, stepping forward. "I know who she is. That's the daughter of the old basket maker—the crazy one who lives by the woods. She bought a hat from me once. The most contrary girl I've ever seen. If everyone else is walking along the road normally, she'll skip backward or stand on her head. If you try to be civil and ask her, 'How are you today?' she'll tell you the entire life cycle of the earthworm." The woman sneered, "Just ignore her lies and stories."

Persimmony was furious. What was wrong with standing on her head occasionally? It helped her see things more clearly. And if she had spent the day watching earthworms, then why shouldn't she talk about them when someone asked? And she was *not* lying about the giant.

"The crazy basket maker's daughter?" the spice merchant cut in. "Well, that explains it. She is *Simeon Smudge's* daughter."

Those standing nearby looked at each other and burst out laughing once again, jabbing their neighbors with their elbows.

"Do you remember when Baldy's old goat kicked

over an applecart and charged into the middle of a group of schoolchildren? Simeon yelled, 'Look out, look out, the goat is loose!' and leaped right onto its back. Oh, my whiskers! I can still see that angry goat trying to shake Simeon off its horns, careening through the streets, trampling on the apples, and charging headlong into a dozen lacy bedsheets hanging up to dry!"

"We all ate a lot of applesauce that month."

"Ha-ha! Or the year when he tried to convince everyone that the poison-tongued jumping tortoises and restless mangroves were going to invade Candlenut?"

"Oh, that was nothing. Remember what happened when he thought all the stars were going to fall into the sea at once and cause a tidal wave to flood the island? Ha! It figures his daughter would be just like him. A giant under the mountain! So like a Smudge."

"Come to think of it, I haven't seen him for years. No wonder things have been peaceful for so long."

Persimmony's cheeks blushed with shame, and her eyes burned. A hundred retorts rose in her throat and got tangled up there, so that she was left sputtering and speechless. But if there is anything worse than a wounded dignity, it is a wounded dignity sitting in a pool of egg yolk. So she left the rude townspeople, stomped over to the overturned pile of crates, and helped the Leafeaters to their feet, picking broken shells off their long green robes as she did so.

The older one thanked her with grim politeness, as if the words tasted bitter in his mouth, but the other clasped her hand. "You lovely girl, how can we repay your kindness?"

"Shhh!" she whispered. "I overheard the two of you talking in the woods a few nights ago. I know the Leafeaters are digging into the mountain to find gold. Wait—let me finish. It's not gold, it's a giant. The archaeologist discovered a belt buckle underneath the castle, and I really did see the giant's head in a cave on the Western Shore, I promise. And now the king's soldiers are going to the Willow Woods to make war, and you've got to help me stop the rest of the Leafeaters before it's too late."

"Young lady, don't you know that eavesdropping is rude?" said Rhedgrave gruffly.

"I had no choice! I was lying inside the tree you were sitting on. It was all the tortoise's fault."

"Well, you have obviously been sent by the king to trick us into calling off the digging. It won't work." Like all the Leafeaters she had ever seen, Rhedgrave's face might have been carved out of the bark of a tree—in his case, a very old coconut tree, rough and scarred by time, but without any of the sweetness. He stood so straight that she thought a sudden wind would snap him in half.

Rheuben, on the other hand, had a face like a white poplar, pale but smooth and strong and fresh. His dark green eyes shone like deep pools as they stared hard into Persimmony's. "But Uncle, I believe she speaks the truth. It is our duty to put right what is going very, very wrong! The diggers are digging straight toward the giant's feet and will surely wake him up!"

Persimmony was impressed. He had figured it out without a philosopher.

"So you see why you have to help me stop them?"

"Of course!" cried Rheuben. "We must get to the woods immediately!"

Relief flooded into her; she still had one question that begged to be asked, and Rheuben's eyes were kind. "I—I have to ask you something," she said hesitantly, almost shyly. "Did you ever kidnap a man named Simeon Smudge? He may have looked a little like me. But taller." She thought for a moment. "And not wearing a dress."

Rhedgrave's impeccably straight face twisted with anger. "You too? How many times do we have to say that Leafeaters never *kidnap* anyone? Why would we want any of your kind polluting our beautiful city?"

Rheuben looked uncomfortably at his uncle and then patted Persimmony's hand kindly. "I'm sorry, but there's no one like you in Willowroot. No Sun-

spitters at all. And certainly no one named Simeon."

"Hey!" yelled someone in the crowd. "That girl is *helping* the Leafeaters!"

"Young lady, you should be ashamed of yourself," the magistrate scolded. "Go home immediately and ask for a good spanking. And you two," he growled to Rheuben and Rhedgrave, "aren't going anywhere

except a jail cell." He yelled to those standing nearby, "Tomorrow they will stand trial."

"Quick! How do I find the entrance to your city?" Persimmony said frantically as arms reached out to grab the two Leafeaters.

"Rheuben," said Rhedgrave in a warning tone, "don't—"

"Look for one of the very large willow trees, with a knot protruding from the side of the trunk," Rheuben whispered. "Those are our door handles. They are scattered throughout the forest."

"That's it? Is there a trick to it? A key, or a password, or—?"

Rheuben looked back at her earnestly as the magistrate pulled him away. "Remember your manners!" he cried, and disappeared behind the crowd.

Chapter 15

In Which It Is Better to Be a Noble Worm Than a Dead Frog (Or Something Like That)

The second day in the pepper mill was the same as the first. But at lunchtime, when the workers escaped to the fresh air for a few brief minutes, Mrs. Smudge and Prunella overheard a conversation between two men who were huddled behind them, munching their stale bread and talking in whispers.

"Tonight will be the night when it will all become too much to bear, and I will cast myself down from the tower window onto the earth below!" The speaker broke off with a little choked sob.

"Don't be silly, Ned," said his companion gruffly.

"We can't have everyone jumping out of windows. The king would just send his foreman out into the villages again and force more innocent people to work here. Oh, the injustice! Someone should rise up and rebel against this terrible tyranny once and for all."

"Yes," Ned agreed. "Someone should."

"And there's no better time than now. A rumor has spread around the island that there is gold buried underneath the castle and that the king has had all of his dungeons dug up in order to find it. If there are no dungeons, then no one can be thrown into prison. And now there's another reward to be had—gold. Not that one's motivation should be to gain riches, of course," he added quickly, a shadow of doubt crossing his face. "It would mean taking from the king what doesn't belong to him anyway and giving it to people who need it. Feeding starving turnip farmers is a noble cause, right? Perhaps not like saving the endangered seven-winged singing mosquito, but—"

"I have never heard of a more noble cause in my life."

"Yes," sighed Flack. "Someone should do it."

"Someone should, you're right," agreed Ned.

Mrs. Smudge had heard enough. She threw down her bread crusts, grabbed Prunella by the wrist, and slipped back to where the men were sitting. "What are we waiting for? We've got to figure out a plan to rebel."

"Excuse me, ma'am," said Flack, blinking his eyes and looking around, "but do you mean us?"

"Of course I mean you. Both of you, and both of us, and whoever will follow after us. What's the good of a noble cause if you don't do anything about it?"

Flack blinked again. "You have a point."

"But rebelling would be dangerous!" said Ned.

"My dear, kind, generous, stupid young peacock," said Mrs. Smudge, "I hate this miserable mill with a hatred so great that my fingers and toes tingle with the desire to tear it down stone by stone and throw every pinch of pepper into the great blue ocean, and what I would like to do to that sneering Mr. Fulcrumb is far too shocking for my sweet Prunella's delicate ears to hear. If I have to march right up to the castle and give the king himself a good spanking, well, all I can say is—you can always count on a Smudge."

"But your daughter," Ned persisted. "Surely you wouldn't send *her* into such danger?"

"Oh please, Mother," Prunella whispered, "let's forget about this whole thing. The pepper mill isn't so bad, really. There's actually a lovely view from the top."

"Did you say *Smudge*?" Flack asked sharply. "You're not related to Simeon Smudge, are you?"

"I am his wife," Mrs. Smudge said proudly. "And this is his daughter Miss Prunella Smudge, and her younger sister, Persimmony, has been captured, just as we were, I am sure of it, though she doesn't seem to be in the pepper mill. But as soon as we get to that castle and I've finished giving the king a spanking, I'm going to make him tell me where he has put her, and if he has hurt one hair on her dirty little head, he'll be sorry!"

"Forget it," said Flack. "I am not attempting any rescue with a *Smudge*. Impossible. No way."

"Why not?" asked Ned.

"You're too young to remember—you were still playing with toys back then, Ned. Everyone knew Simeon Smudge. He was a peppercorn picker. One day when he was dumping his bag of peppercorns into the grinder, he thought he heard the cry of a child deep down below. And so he made everyone stop turning the wheel until someone could lower him into the grinder to find the child. But the rope broke and he fell in. So another worker was lowered down on a rope, but *he* fell in. And by the time old Fulcrumb found us, half a dozen workers were swimming in pepper, and the rest of us were standing there with broken ropes getting no work done. Turns out all the fuss was over a little bird that had flown into the works, and our lunches were cut in half for a month as punishment!"

"My poor, brave, reckless, unlucky, darling husband," said Mrs. Smudge. "He always knew the world needed to be saved from something; he just had trouble figuring out *what*, that's all. Maybe everything did go wrong when he tried to save people, but at least he tried! Not like *some* people, who sit around all day talking about 'noble causes' instead of being noble. But it's obvious you are cowards, and I have a deep and abiding moral objection to cowardice in all forms. So, good day!" She began to turn her back on them.

"Wait!" said Flack. He looked at her doubtfully. "I assume, then, that you also have a moral objection to injustice, oppression, tyranny, prejudice against turnips, cruelty to animals, and overcooked eggs?"

"*Especially* overcooked eggs."

Flack was silent for a few moments. "Ned, I believe I like Smudges. In fact, I don't know why I never thought of rebelling before. Why *not* us? Why not, after all? We've got brains. We've got strength. We've got an all-consuming desire to do good in this world. So I say, let's do it!"

"Hear, hear!" said Ned.

"Be quiet, you ninny," shushed Mrs. Smudge. "Do you want to give our plans away?"

"But we don't have any plans yet," whispered Flack.

So they put their heads together—at least Flack, Ned, and Mr. Smudge put their heads together, while Prunella buried her head in her apron—and came up with a scheme to free the pepper mill workers. Then the conspirators climbed back up the stairs to the top of the pepper mill, took their places again at the wheel, and waited eagerly for the right moment to put their plan into action.

Persimmony raced past the pepper mill along the road leading to the Willow Woods. She knew she had to hurry—there was no telling how close the Leafeater diggers were to the giant's feet—and yet something held her back. Gradually the road faded into grass and dirt, and she ran more and more slowly, until at last she trudged with a heavy heart. And as she paused to take a breath, she saw to her right, tucked behind a tangle of bushes, her own cottage.

It looked so small and vulnerable. A giant could blow it over gently with a breath. But it belonged to a world in which there were no giants, no soldiers, and no Leafeaters with disastrous plans—only dirty dishes, baskets made of sea grass and palm leaves, and quarrels with Prunella. She could walk through that door and receive the punishment coming to her, and do her chores, and go to bed, and forget the creature in the cave and the painful lump inside of her that wouldn't go away.

She hesitated, but only for a moment. "Mother! Prunella!" She ran into the cottage. The broom lay on the grass outside the window. The broken pieces of the Giving Pot were gathered in a corner by the fireplace. The willow wands and branches waited in neat piles.

Grabbing the quilt from her bed, Persimmony climbed down the ladder to the little cellar underneath the cottage and sat amidst the jars and the musty old blankets, with the basket from the cave beside her. For the first time since her journey started, she wanted to cry. She pulled the quilt over her head and tried very hard, but no tears would come out. *Brave of heart and light of foot* . . . Adventures were so much simpler when they happened inside her head.

Everyone had laughed at him—*her* father. They had laughed as if he was just a silly man instead of the hero she knew he must be. How could they do that? It was like laughing at a giant. It was like a mighty giant had shrunk to the size of an earthworm. She didn't want her father to be an earthworm. She put her head on her knees and pressed the ends of her hair against her closed eyelids.

Ever since the cave, she had been secretly hoping that she would find her father in the Leafeater city, and they would stop the Leafeaters together, and he would help her make everyone believe because he had seen the giant too. But Rhedgrave Rhinkle had said that the Leafeaters never kidnapped anyone, and

Rheuben Rhinkle had said there was no one in Willowroot like her. The Rhinkles could have been lying, of course. If they had actually kidnapped someone, would they *admit* it? But Rheuben had believed her. And she believed him.

Where was her father, then? Perhaps he—perhaps—

Perhaps he had passed her in a crowd of people and not recognized her, because she was just an ordinary little girl who had never done anything worth noticing. Perhaps he had snuck up to the cottage one day, peeked through the window, taken one look at her, and decided not to come back after all.

On the other hand, she thought more practically, perhaps he had taken one look at Prunella.

There was only one possibility left that she could think of: He had never made it out of the cave. She remembered the giant's teeth, glimmering in the faint light of the torch. She remembered the quivering and quaking of his enormous mouth as he dreamed. If someone got too close . . .

This was too much. This was unbearable. She shook herself as if she were waking up from a nightmare. But the nightmare wasn't over yet.

Where were her mother and sister? Maybe she should go and find them. They could fill this cellar with apples and berries, and stay here until the danger had passed. The giant might stomp the cottage to bits, but they would be safe under the ground. But what if she didn't find them in time?

What was Worvil doing? She remembered what he had said: "I wonder what it's like to be eaten." Ugh! Sometimes she wished she didn't have *quite* such a good imagination.

There was no stopping the worst from happening unless someone stopped the Leafeaters from digging. What if—?

She reached into the basket and picked up the little pine-needle creations and turned them over and over in her hands. And now she realized what the second one was: a grasshopper, with little twigs for legs and wings covered with silvery, wispy strands of a spiderweb. A turtle and a grasshopper. He had taken them with him into the cave—why? To remind him of her and Prunella? To give himself courage to face a giant for their sake?

Her father wasn't a failure. He had saved twelve starfish from a hungry sea otter.

He was brave. He wouldn't have hidden under a quilt when his family was in danger. If he saw her now, would he be proud of her?

Persimmony threw off the quilt. There was a

kingdom to save. She climbed back up to the cottage and began filling her father's basket with whatever bits of food she could find. A little water jug on the floor had a dead frog inside, but she dumped it out and filled the jug with water. She was about to throw the dead frog out the window, but changed her mind and put it on Prunella's pillow. There—things felt a little bit normal again. Smiling, she set her face toward the woods.

Chapter 16

IN WHICH CAPTAIN GIDDING SHOWS HIS VALOR WITH COCONUTS

And so Persimmony was back where she had started only two nights ago. She climbed through the bushes to the dirt path that led into the Willow Woods and all the way to the potter's cottage. Only this time, the woods were silent—and she was careful to stay on the path.

Her plan was to stick close to the potter's cottage and walk in wider and wider circles looking for one of the large willows that Rheuben had described. When she arrived at the cottage, however, she found it occupied. The king's soldiers had been given no directions for how to find Willowroot—since of course no one knew were it was—and so they had come here, to the only place in the woods where they had been before. They had already lost one of their number—a soldier had sat down in a patch of poison ivy and had run screaming and itching all the way back up Mount Majestic.

Captain Gidding was walking around the cottage, sniffing wildflowers and peering into gopher holes. It was his first time outside the castle in ten years (usually his job was to be the king's personal bodyguard, which meant standing outside the royal bedroom and swatting mosquitoes at night), and therefore he was in ecstasy over everything around him. He spotted Persimmony and ran to greet her with his arms full of white and yellow blossoms. "Do you smell that?" he cried. "It is the sweet aroma of honeysuckle. Is there anything more lovely in all the world?"

Captain Gidding's face was so open and honest. Persimmony knew that, even if he didn't believe her, *he* at least would not laugh at her. She untied the hair belt from around her waist and told him everything she had seen.

Slowly the excitement in Captain Gidding's eyes turned to quiet awe. He took the giant's hair in his hands, stroking it reverently. "To think that we live in a world where such a being exists! Doesn't the island seem *bigger* to you all of a sudden, knowing that it contains a giant?"

Persimmony had not thought about this. She was too busy thinking about what the island would be like if everything on it were squashed flat. "Then you believe me?"

The captain looked at her as if she had asked a nonsensical question. "Of course!"

"Then you see why I've got to find the Leafeaters and tell them as soon as possible to stop digging into the mountain?"

"Brave girl, you have looked upon a creature whose presence would have shattered the hearts of most grown men. I will follow you to the depths of the earth if I can serve you in this worthy quest."

Persimmony felt as if every heroic tale she had ever told herself under the quilt at night was suddenly bursting out into the daylight.

"Then find something that will make marks on the trees and let's start searching," she said. "We don't have much time left before—"

She was interrupted by a cry of rapture from Captain Gidding. "A buttermilk-blue-dappled butterfly! I never believed that I should live to see such a thing. Oh, there it goes!"

"That's nice, Captain Gidding, but did you hear what I said? We need to hurry . . . Captain Gidding, where are you going? Stop!" The captain was rapidly disappearing into the trees—still holding the giant's hair. The other eleven soldiers, seeing their superior take off with such speed, obediently jumped up and followed. "Wait!" cried Persimmony. "You've got my hair!" And she ran after them.

It was nearly dusk when Mr. Fulcrumb began to climb the pepper mill stairs to check on his workers, as he did every evening. He went slowly, loudly, knowing that above him they were all trembling at the sound of his approach.

And all were—except four. Flack, Ned, Mrs. Smudge, and Prunella heard the footsteps and looked at one another across the crowded room. Mrs. Smudge winked.

Mr. Fulcrumb reached the top of the stairs and stopped beside his assistant to survey the workers. They were a lovely picture, soaked in sweat with their hair plastered to their foreheads like that. "Faster! Faster!" he yelled.

Mrs. Smudge stumbled out of line. She clutched her heart, spun around twice, and collapsed onto the floor.

Prunella shrieked and rushed to her side.

Mr. Fulcrumb didn't move. "Get back to work."

Prunella threw her clothespin across the room and cried out, "You've killed her! You've killed her! Oh, Mother, darling Mother, don't leave me here in this wretched place with this horrible man. Aaaaaachooo!"

"GET BACK TO WORK!" Mr. Fulcrumb said.

But Prunella sobbed and Prunella wailed and Prunella sneezed and Prunella blubbered, until not a person in the room could bear the sound of her suffering a moment longer . . . for if there was one talent in the world Prunella possessed, it was a gift for going into hysterics.

The grinder slowed. The other workers paused and turned to see what was happening. Ned and Flack emerged from the shadows.

Mr. Fulcrumb walked over to where Prunella sat beside Mrs. Smudge. "Did you hear be? I said . . . get . . . back . . . to . . . WORK!!!!"

Flack jumped forward and grabbed the foreman's arms from behind. Mrs. Smudge came alive and grabbed his feet. The foreman's loyal assistant ran to the aid of his boss, but Ned stuck out one leg to trip him, and the assistant landed flat on his nose. The rest of the mill workers, realizing at last that a rebellion was underfoot, left their places at the grinder with a joyful cheer and joined the fight. "Tie theb up," Flack yelled. In a matter of seconds, Mr. Fulcrumb and his assistant were back to back, bound together with rope.

"You'll be arrested for treasod!" Mr. Fulcrumb screamed. "You'll be throwd idto the kig's dudgeons! You'll be eated alive by rats! You'll be hugg upside dowd by your toedails!"

But his screams went unheard amidst the cheering of the crowd as the men hoisted the wriggling bundle above their shoulders and sprinted down the stairs—sluggish no more. The workers burst out of the door of the pepper mill into the fresh air and followed Flack to the back of the mill, where he opened the chute and let the pepper pour out onto the ground. "Bag it up! Bag it up!" he said, and the workers who had followed him scooped up the pepper into large sacks. When the chute was clear, Flack and Ned lifted up the two squirming captives, stuck them inside, and shut the door again, not forgetting to take off the foreman's clothespin.

Flack didn't waste a moment. He climbed onto the wooden cart that was now loaded with sacks of pepper and turned to face the liberated mill workers. "By fellow citizeds," he said proudly, "we are dot goig to put up with this tyraddy ady logger!"

"HEAR, HEAR!" shouted the crowd.

"Are we ready to give His Highdess Kig Lucas a taste of his owd bedicine?"

"YES!" cheered the crowd.

"Thed follow be!" And with that, Flack jumped off the cart and began marching toward Mount Majestic.

"Let's go!" yelled Mrs. Smudge, pulling Prunella behind her.

"But I thought we were looking for Persimmony!" said Prunella, who had lost her clothespin and didn't care. "Can't the bad men just say they're sorry and we can all go home?"

"*Prudella Sbudge!*"

"Yes, Mother."

If Prunella was confused as she followed her mother, Persimmony was even more confused as she, Captain Gidding, and the soldiers ran after the buttermilk-blue-dappled butterfly in the Willow Woods. It led them toward the mountain; it led them toward the sea; it led them up into trees and down again; it led them around and around and around in circles.

When Persimmony finally caught up with the group, her words tumbled over each other: "Thanks to you we are now completely lost! — Oh, my hat! —

Stop that, quickly!" For she had noticed three things at once.

First, she noticed that Captain Gidding was crouching before a gorgeous creature with creamy wings speckled with blue.

Second, she noticed that the butterfly was perched on top of her very own hat that had flown away in the thunderstorm. Apparently the butterfly thought it was an apple tree.

Third, she noticed that they were in a grove of coconut palms and willow trees and that the soldiers were attacking the long willow boughs with their swords. A bird in the branches had dropped something white and sticky on the head of one of their fellows, and they were trying bring the offending creature to justice.

Persimmony yelled to the soldiers again. They dropped their swords in surprise at the urgency in her voice.

But it was too late. The willows had been disturbed. Down crawled the poison-tongued jumping tortoises, sliding slowly from the tree trunks surrounding the little party. There was no chance of hiding or running this time. Four, five—no, six tortoises crept forward, tightening the circle slowly.

Then one of the poison-tongued jumping tortoises pounced.

A soldier drew his sword, but the tortoise already had him on the ground, flattened underneath a massive shell with a poisonous tongue aimed straight at his nose. Suddenly the willow grove was a battlefield. Swords were useless against the spiked armor

of the tortoises, but the soldiers swung them wildly anyway. The beasts jumped after the men, who dodged left and right—and the air was filled with the thud of metal against tortoise shells and the thud of tortoise shells against tree trunks.

Persimmony grabbed the sword the first fallen soldier had dropped and drove it into the foot of the nearest tortoise. The tortoise turned with an angry hiss. The world around her spun wildly. There was a sharp pain in her chest as she fell under the weight of the furious creature and felt its muscular legs pressing all of the breath out of her. She pushed her arms against the heavy flanks with all her might, but she was not strong enough. The tortoise's tongue was inches from her face.

Suddenly a blade flashed in front of her eyes, and the severed tongue flew out of the tortoise's mouth into the bushes. The tortoise screamed in agony and drew its head and limbs into its shell.

"Get up!" said Captain Gidding anxiously, sheathing his sword and rolling the huge tortoise off Persimmony. "Run! Find a place to hide. I'll take care of these devils."

Persimmony watched dumbfounded as the captain, whose mind had just been full of honeysuckle and butterflies, swiftly leaped back into the fray. "The coconuts! Use the coconuts!" he yelled, picking up one of the many fallen coconuts that lay in the grass and hurling it at a tortoise. It hit the beast directly on the snout, and the tortoise withdrew into its shell. The rest of the castle guard began to do the same, and soon there was a blur of flying coconuts.

Persimmony did not hide. She raced around the grove, loading her arms with coconuts and heaving them at every tortoise she saw. Her fear was gone now. This was the moment she had been waiting for. This was what adventures were all about. She ran, she threw, she jumped, she dodged—

And then her head struck something tall and stubborn, and the world went black.

Chapter 17

In Which Injustice Is Overthrown and a Perfectly Good Bubble Bath Is Spoiled

After the soldiers had departed for the Willow Woods and Persimmony, Worvil, and Guaf-noggle had departed for the Snoring Cave, King Lucas had (true to his word) spent most of that day taking bubble baths, until he was finally able to thrust archeologists, professors, potters, giants, milk, and rude girls out of his mind completely.

But angry pepper mill workers have a knack for thrusting themselves into one's mind, and into one's bathroom. The door came off its hinges and clattered to the ground, and fifty pairs of feet stomped in. Lucas stared at the intruders and quickly sank low beneath the bubbles, but a bathtub was no escape. The rebels brought forward several huge sacks and emptied each one into the bathwater with a loud "hurrah!" until Lucas was buried up to his ears in soggy pepper and sneezing uncontrollably.

"H-h-how da-ha-ha-haaaaaaaaCHOOOO! dare you!! I hereby arrest all of you for treason and condemn you to-to-horrible pu-hu-hu-ACHOOO-OOOOOOO punishments forever!"

Flack reached up and took the clothespin off his nose, and the rest of the crowd did the same as ceremoniously as if they were lowering their weapons on command. Lucas glanced toward a chair in the corner where his clothes were lying. Mrs. Smudge, following his eyes, grabbed the king's clothes and triumphantly hung them on a peg far away from the bathtub. The rebels broke into laughter. Prunella turned bright red. "Mother," she whispered, "if you put them over there, the king can't get dressed!"

"That's the point," hissed Mrs. Smudge.

Prunella shook her head miserably. She supposed this was the sort of thing Persimmony would call an "adventure," and that made her even more certain that she would never understand it.

Flack continued, "You see, Your Highness, you have no choice but to listen to us. We are your loyal servants of the pepper mill, who have been slaving away in order to give you all the pepper you want. We have now done that. You have all the pepper you want right in front of you. I hope you enjoy it."

"What do you want?"

"Our freedom!" shouted Ned.

"No! You've got to keep making pepper! I need

pepper! Except that I need it on my food, not in my bathtub."

"Then fire Mr. Fulcrumb," demanded Flack.

"Done," said Lucas.

"And apologize for how selfish you've been."

Lucas fumed and squirmed and writhed in his bathtub. But with fifty angry (and clothed) subjects surrounding him with more sacks of pepper held in waiting, and no one around to protect him, there was very little he could do. "Mmssrry," he mumbled.

"What?"

"I'm sorry!" Lucas snapped.

"And now give us your gold in return for all the pain and suffering you've caused us."

Lucas paused. "What gold?"

"The gold you have been digging for underneath the castle."

"How do you know about that?"

"The whole kingdom knows about that. No one can keep a secret for long on an island."

Now this was a dilemma indeed. He obviously could not give them *that* gold, since so far there was no gold to give—except for the belt buckle, if it was a belt buckle, and that certainly wasn't going anywhere. "There isn't any gold," Lucas said finally.

"Your Highness, do you actually think we are stupid enough to believe that?" said Flack impatiently. "Now tell us what you have done with the gold, and we'll give you your clothes back and leave you alone."

"I'm telling you, there isn't any gold I can give you." Lucas struggled to stifle a sneeze and pounced on the best story to get this rabble out of his bathroom. "What I thought was gold was really the belt buckle of a giant asleep under Mount Majestic. So you see there is really nothing I can do for you."

Flack turned to Ned. "Empty another sack of pepper over his head."

"No, no!" cried Lucas. "You'll see! There is a search party going to the caves on the Western Shore right now to search for the giant's head and see if he is really there."

Mrs. Smudge's eyes widened and her face turned as purple as the handkerchief on her head. *Caves? Giant?* "Is this a joke? Is this a joke, you deceiving, swindling, pepper-hogging, shoe-wearing . . . big-eared . . ." (she was so astonished she nearly ran out of adjectives) ". . . *short* monarch? Did your father, the late king, put you up to this? Do you mean to mock a poor, honest, heartbroken woman?"

"Well, if it is a joke, it's somebody else's joke, and a dirty girl with a name like Persnickety has gone to find out. But until she comes back, there's no gold to give you!"

And now all the color drained out of Mrs. Smudge's face completely. "You sent Persimmony—*my* Persimmony—to the Snoring Cave?"

"Yes, but—what do you mean *your* Persimmony? Who *are* you? And how did you know it was called the Snoring Cave?"

"What cave, Mother?" whispered Prunella. "Why is Persimmony in a cave?"

Mrs. Smudge did not answer but stood gaping at the king in horror.

"So that's it!" yelled Flack. "You've hidden the gold in the caves and made up a silly story about a giant to scare people away from it. Well, you won't scare us away. Come, comrades! We'll camp out on the mountain tonight, and tomorrow we'll find the gold!" With a deafening cheer, the pepper mill workers swarmed out of the room.

"Not that we're after the treasure for ourselves, of course," added Flack, hanging back. "We're going to give it to the poor. And speaking of the poor, we also need to talk about—"

"Hurry up, you goody-two-boots." Mrs. Smudge seemed to snap out of the spell she was in and come back to herself. She yanked Flack by the arm.

"You haven't heard the last from me!" yelled Flack as he was pulled out of the room.

Prunella stared at the king. She curtsied politely and said, "Pleased to meet you, Your Highness." She was about to take the king's clothes down from the hook to give back to him, when Mrs. Smudge swept back into the room, grabbed her hand, and swept them both out again.

As soon as the coast was clear, the trembling steward stepped into the bathroom. Tucked away behind the wrinkles on his face was the faintest shadow of a smile. "I am so sorry, Your Highness. They overtook us so suddenly, there was nothing anyone could do—between sneezing—to stop them . . ."

"Nubbins," said Lucas, "does Badly still have a cold?"

"What? Oh, er, yes, I do believe he does, Your Highness. We have been giving him every available remedy but—"

"Good! Then he's the only one in the castle who can't smell the pepper if they throw it at him. Send him at once to find the search party on the Western Shore and warn them not to tell the pepper mill workers which cave is the Snoring Cave. Searching every cave for gold should keep those traitors out of my bathroom for a while."

"Yes, sir, I certainly will, Your Highness." The steward turned to go.

"And Nubbins, will you hand me my clothes?"

When Persimmony awoke, the woods were quiet, and the moon was shining brightly in the night sky. Captain Gidding was bending over her, gently bathing her forehead with a wet cloth. Her head lay on something soft. "What happened?" she said.

"We were fighting the poison-tongued jumping tortoises—" he began.

"I remember that part," she said.

"And you leaped bravely into the battle—"

"Yes, I definitely remember that part!"

"And then you ran into a tree."

Persimmony closed her eyes and groaned with shame. Her first real battle, her first chance to show valor, and what did she do? Ran into a tree. If she had been hit on the head with a coconut, at least she could have said she was wounded in the line of duty. She was humiliated. *So like a Smudge.*

"As soon as the tortoises realized we had found a way of hitting them where they were weak, they sucked themselves into their shells and will not be coming out again for many hours, I daresay," Captain Gidding told her.

Persimmony lifted herself up on one elbow. In the dim light of the candle that Captain Gidding had set in the dirt beside them, she could just make out the huge, black, motionless lumps huddled together in the middle of the grove. A few feet away from her on a blanket of moss lay eight soldiers, softly snoring.

The captain read her mind. "Only those eight are left with us. Three returned to the castle. They were badly wounded, but they will live. Oh, they are a brave and loyal lot, they are."

Persimmony did not share his esteem for the king's guard. "But we're lost. How will they find their way back?"

Captain Gidding pointed above the trees. It was a clear night, and against the dark blue of the sky the black outline of Mount Majestic and the faint glimmering lights of the distant castle pointed the way home. Of course. The mountain. The one thing that would always be there. Except that it wouldn't.

Persimmony stretched her arms and legs to make sure everything still worked. She had managed to make it through with only scratches on her chest and shoulders, but they were deep and throbbed painfully. Her dress was torn in two places. The soft pillow she'd been lying on, she now realized, was the thick hair of the giant. She tied it around her waist again. "I didn't expect you to be so good with a sword. Or a coconut, for that matter."

"That's okay. Neither did I." But there was no pride in his voice. Instead, he let out a deep sigh, and Persimmony thought his eyes looked strange, as if he'd been weeping. He sat with his knees pulled up close to his chest and stared out into the night.

"What are you doing?" Persimmony asked.

"I am contemplating the willows," answered the captain. "Why do you think the willows hang their heads and weep?"

"I thought it was the weight of those heavy tortoises sitting on top."

"Weight, yes! They carry the weight of the world on their shoulders. They are the most compassionate of all the trees—so beautiful and so sad."

Persimmony stared at the absentminded, bumbling, courageous man. "I never thought of it that way," she said.

Captain Gidding wiped his eyes and cleared his throat. "I've been sitting here trying to make up a poem about it while you've been unconscious, but I just can't find the right words: *I climbed a hill* as high as hope . . . What should go next? Do you know?"

"No, I don't," said Persimmony, wishing she did because his face was so earnest and pleading.

"Oh well, I will have to keep thinking, then. I suppose you should go to sleep now. You've had quite a bump on the head."

Her head did hurt. Persimmony lay down again and closed her eyes. As she listened to the lullaby of the wind and the snoring of the soldiers, she thought, *Are the willows weeping for me?*

It was many minutes later, or many hours, when a rustling in the leaves woke her again and she opened her eyes halfway. A tall shadow moved in the glade. It was a mangrove tree, crawling slowly across the forest floor until it reached the tortoise shells. It spread its roots out wide so that they became a cage around the tortoises, and there it stood like a guard over its unsuspecting prisoners.

One restless mangrove, at least, had found its place.

Chapter 18

IN WHICH PERSIMMONY REMEMBERS HER MANNERS

"My hat!" Persimmony sat up straight, awake in the quiet woods, with the morning streaming through the branches. Captain Gidding and the soldiers were asleep on the grass.

The hat was still lying on the ground where the buttermilk-blue-dappled butterfly had found it. It had the dirty footprint of a tortoise right in the middle of it, but otherwise it was unharmed. She put it back on her head to help her think. She found her basket in a bush nearby and munched on an apple.

They were lost, that was certain. The butterfly chase had taken so many twists and turns that she had no idea where in the forest they were or how far it was back to the potter's cottage. The only obvious landmark was Mount Majestic, but that wouldn't help them find Willowroot.

The tortoises were awake inside the mangrove's prison of roots, and they were angry. Persimmony couldn't resist: She stuck out her tongue and wiggled her fingers. A spiky shell threw itself toward her against the thick roots and bounced back. She danced around and around the tree. *Come after me now!* she silently mouthed to the captive snouts. Then she noticed that one of the tortoises had not come out of its shell yet, and she guessed that it was the one whose tongue had been cut out. Now it was too ashamed to show its face to the world.

And then she felt a little sorry for teasing them. But she couldn't sit still, and she didn't want to wake up the soldiers, so she decided to walk in a wide circle around the grove, slowly making her way farther and farther out. She carefully inspected each willow tree, pushing every knot or bump she could see, pulling on roots, kicking the trunks. Nothing. Then one tree standing at a distance from the others caught her eye. It was very large, and its branches fell so thickly that they seemed to form a wall of green stretching upward as far as her eyes could see.

She parted them gently with her hands and stepped underneath the canopy of leaves into a still and silent place. The trunk was twice as wide as she was tall, and on its side was one knotty lump. She grasped it, but it would not move.

Remember your manners, Rheuben had told her. What did that mean? Should she curtsy? She did so, not very well, and felt very silly with only a tree in front of her. But nothing happened. Frustration welled up inside of her, but she pressed it down again and tried to remember what she had heard that night after the storm.

Yes, please, Rheuben had replied, and then they had gone.

No—that wasn't quite right. There had been a pause between his words. *Yes,* he had said to Rhedgrave, then—

"Please!" Persimmony said. Still nothing happened. But just to make sure, she grasped the knot again and twisted it. It turned, and the side of the tree opened outward to reveal a narrow dirt staircase spiraling down into darkness.

"I found it," she whispered. Then she shouted joyfully, "I've found the entrance to Willowroot!"

In a moment, the wall of branches parted again

and Captain Gidding was beside her, followed by eight groggy, bleary-eyed soldiers. "Marvelous!" the captain cheered. "Brilliant! You are the bravest *and* cleverest girl I have ever had the pleasure of meeting. You are destined for great things, Miss Smudge."

Persimmony's heart began to feel lighter. Even "Smudge" sounded noble when he said it like that. If only Captain Gidding had been there when the people of Candlenut had made fun of her.

"Ugh!" grumbled one of the soldiers, peering down the hole. "Who knows what worms and termites and muddy goo might be waiting for us."

"You don't have to follow me, then," said Persimmony curtly. "I'll go by myself."

"Send a young lady alone into unknown underground perils?" said the soldier. "Never. Leave all the danger to us."

"Not likely," muttered Persimmony as she descended into the darkness.

The staircase was steep, damp, and smelled like rotting leaves. It also curved, as Persimmony found out the hard way when her foot hit the wall and she slipped downward several steps. She could hear the soldiers behind her struggling to squeeze their clumsy arms and legs into the cramped space and complaining loudly of the dampness. Finally the steps ended, and she moved forward into the open space beyond, blinking while her eyes adjusted to the dim light of candles.

The stairs had led her down into some kind of underground storeroom where there were piles of leaves, neatly sorted and stacked according to kind, shape, and size. On the opposite side of the storeroom from the stairs was a wooden door, which Persimmony opened eagerly. She caught her breath in awe.

She was in what appeared to be a large meeting hall. The roof was curved like an upside-down bowl. There were many other doorways as well, some small like the one she had just come through, while others were larger and nestled under high arches of painted vines woven together.

Persimmony barely noticed these things, however, for what made her catch her breath was the feeling that she was back aboveground again. The walls were elaborately painted with glorious pictures of trees. There were coconut palms bent sideways from the wind. There were clusters of mangrove trees as they grew at the forest's edge along the shore. And there were stately willows with boughs drooping to the ground like green waterfalls.

The dome above was painted to look like the sky,

with the sun and moon and stars. Farther down were hundreds of pictures stretching in a circle around the room—pictures of Mount Majestic, of fields ripe for harvest and orchards ripe for picking, of fishing boats on the sea and brown seals on the rocks, of goats and squirrels and pelicans.

And most of all, there were pictures of Leafeaters, with arms and legs growing like crooked branches out of their green robes. One such figure on the wall nearest to her was so lifelike and looked so stern that Persimmony had to touch it to make sure it was only a picture.

She felt as if she were seeing the island for the very first time. But what would it look like if the giant awoke? Would the mangrove trees run into the ocean? Would the green orchards lie smashed in a mess of leaves and spoiled fruit? Would the giant be so tall he would block the sun?

"There must be something here," mused Captain Gidding, gazing at the walls in wonder, "some clue to where we should go. In the best works of art, you can't always figure out the meaning immediately. Sometimes your heart knows first, even while your mind is still lost."

"We've been around the whole room," said Persimmony, "and there is no picture of the Leafeaters digging a tunnel through the mountain, and no map of the city."

The captain looked around a bit nervously. "I . . . I think we should go through one of the biggest doorways, with the arches of vines above them."

"Why?"

"Because they're so beautiful."

The vines painted along the bottom of the walls and over the arches were indeed very beautiful, but Persimmony didn't see what that had to do with finding a way through the city. "Well, that still leaves four doors to choose from."

"I think we should take one as far as it goes, and hopefully along the way we'll meet someone who can give us directions," said one soldier.

"I think we should bang our swords together until they hear us and come running, and then we'll attack them," said another.

"I think," said Persimmony, "that everyone should take a different doorway. By lunchtime we'll all meet back here and tell the others what we found. But we'll wear disguises so the Leafeaters won't recognize us and we can follow them secretly to the place where they're digging. And then we can take off our disguises and rush at them all at once with our swords raised, yelling, 'STOP DIGGING, IN THE NAME

OF THE KING! THERE'S A GIANT UNDER THERE!' And they'll be so surprised they'll drop their shovels and surrender."

Captain Gidding and the soldiers stared at her with something a little like awe.

"The rest can split up," said the captain, "but you and I will go together. I have sworn to protect you. You might never find your way back out again, and then how would I explain to the king that I lost one of his subjects?"

"He would probably give you a medal of honor."

"But how are we going to disguise ourselves?" asked one of the soldiers.

Persimmony smiled. "I have an idea."

Chapter 19

IN WHICH THE RUMBLEBUMPS INVENT A NEW GAME AND WORVIL GAINS PERSPECTIVE

Around the same time that Persimmony awoke in the woods, Worvil was awakened by a drop of water falling on his chin. His head ached. Rumblebumps, with their thick hair and many layers of clothing, had little need for mattresses or pillows or blankets, but Worvil's night on the cold stone floor of the cliff-side cave had been as comfortable as sleeping on a lump of ice, and about as wet.

He also had indigestion. It was hard enough to be forced out of politeness (and fear of starvation) to eat a seven-course meal of seaweed cooked and served in every imaginable fashion. But then all the Rumblebump children had taken turns playing leap-frog over his head, and the women had swung him around helplessly in a wild dance despite his pro-tests, and Guafnoggle had picked him up and carried him through the surf to bob and sputter in a freezing ocean while the rest of the Rumblebumps swam in a mirror of stars and Sallyroo chased the reflection of the moon, hoping to catch it in her pocket.

Worvil was certain that his stomach had perma-nently turned upside down, and he definitely felt a case of Green Intestinitis Agoniosis coming on. He wondered if Persimmony was worrying yet.

He sat up very carefully and tested his stiff neck to make sure it would still bend upward (the most important movement for seeing a giant in time to escape). Around him on the floor were the rem-nants of last night's most solemn activity, if anything the Rumblebumps did could be called "solemn": A crown of seaweed had been passed on to him by the previous Grand Stomper. The little orange starfish itself was lying innocently in a conch shell filled with sea water.

Oh, how he hated that starfish! And yet, if he hadn't found it, then he never would have been able to stop the Rumblebumps from waking the giant.

The rest of the cave was filled from wall to wall with sleeping Rumblebumps curled up on top of each other like rabbits. Hoping to find some form of breakfast other than seaweed, Worvil tiptoed past his new followers and out of the cave. The warm, salty air hit his face.

There, sitting on a rock only a few feet away from the cave, a wet, bedraggled figure was sobbing uncontrollably. Normally Worvil would never have dared to approach a stranger, but then again, anyone more miserable than Worvil was surely not too much of a threat.

The young man jumped at the touch of Worvil's tentative hand on his shoulder. As he looked up, Worvil saw that his nose was red and swollen. "Oh sure, go ahead," said the stranger. "Pick od be. Igdore by udhealthy coddition. Forget that I've got a bessage frob the kig. Just throw be back id the sea agaid, add baybe I'll just float away for good." He held a soggy handkerchief to his nose and blew. The blast made Worvil jump and scared away a flock of pigeons that had been sunning nearby.

For it was poor Badly, and if anyone had had a worse night than Worvil, it was he. In between blasts into the handkerchief, and with a lot of repeating, he managed to explain that he had been sent to warn the

Rumblebumps that an army of pepper mill workers had attacked the king and was coming to the Western Shore. On the way, however, he had been overtaken by the rebels themselves, who thought he was a spy and held him captive the entire night for questioning. After they found that torturing him with pepper had no effect on his clogged nostrils, they dragged him down the cliffs and tossed him into the water, leaving him to swim back on his own. He'd been shivering and sobbing ever since.

"But where are they now?" cried Worvil.

Badly pointed to the left, and Worvil could just see in the distance a large group of people scurrying over the rocks in different directions. "They're searchig all the caves lookig for gold."

Worvil's upside-down stomach turned inside out, split into a dozen pieces, and started a civil war.

He ran back into the Rumblebumps' cave. "Wake up! Danger! Threat! Emergency! Oh, what shall we do? What shall we do?" The Rumblebumps didn't need to be told twice. The threat of danger didn't bother them, but it was always so much fun to wake up, after all. They jumped up and nearly flattened Worvil to the ground in their excitement to get out of the cave and into the morning light. Sallyroo came out carrying the conch shell. "Grand

Stomper, you've forgotten your starfish," she cried happily, thrusting it into Worvil's trembling hands. "Don't you remember you have to carry it *every-where* for a whole week, and then you throw it back to the sea!"

"Listen to me!" said Worvil, and they did.

"Yes, Grand Stomper?" said Guafnoggle when Worvil hesitated.

Worvil gulped. "There's a big problem. A really big problem. Do you see that group of people way over there jumping around on the rocks? They're trying to — I mean, they — " He stopped again. How in the world was he going to make the Rumble-bumps understand how serious this situation was? "They're trying to find the Snoring Cave, and — and it's *very* important that we stop them from finding it!"

Guafnoggle's eyes lit up. "You mean like a *game?*" The Rumblebumps burst into cheers. "Go, Grand Stomper! Go, Grand Stomper! Go, Grand Stomper . . ."

"*Shhhh!*" Worvil saw one of the searchers lift his head at the noise and look in the direction of the Rumblebumps. "Yes, yes, it's a game. Whatever you do, *don't let them into the Snoring Cave.*"

The Rumblebumps began discussing the rules of the game in voices much louder than Worvil wished. It was finally decided that ten points would be awarded for stepping on the foot of one of the pepper mill workers, five points for getting one to fall into a tide pool, and two points for tying one up with seaweed.

By the time they finished talking, the pepper mill workers were crawling over the rocks toward them like clumsy cockroaches. The Rumblebumps stomped their feet in a kind of jolly war dance, waving seaweed in their hands. Worvil tiptoed back to the cave where he had slept and grabbed one of the lit torches that hung on the cave wall. The Rumblebumps roared and charged the opposite team. Mixed with the spray of the breakers, a spicy black cloud rose from the crowd, and Worvil (who was allergic to pepper) felt the tickling, burning tempest of a monumental sneeze rush toward his nose. One hand held the conch shell with the starfish in it; the other held the torch. He put down the shell, clapped his free hand over his nose, and ran in the direction of the Snoring Cave.

Guard it with your life, Persimmony had told him. *Guard it with your life.* "I'm a giant in a shrinking body . . . no, I'm the body of a shrinking giant . . . no, no, what did she say? I'm a short person about to burst?"

Behind him he could hear the sounds of a very bizarre battle, with *oooofs* and *aaarghs* interrupted by loud splashes, billows of laughter, and an occasional sneeze. As he reached the Snoring Cave and ducked inside, however, he heard one loud, mournful "Aaaaaaiiiiiiaaa!" drown out the rest. There was a scurry and a shuffle, and then all was silent.

Thinking that the game was over and the Rumblebumps had won, he peeked out of the cave. A sharp-eyed woman with disheveled hair and a striped handkerchief hanging off her left ear peered back at him. "There he is, there's the scrawny one!" she yelled to the crowd of bruised faces emerging from the rocks behind her. "That must be the right cave. Light a torch. Come on! Prunella, you stay out here."

Worvil shrank back into the shelter of the cave. Here was a lifetime of nightmares coming together in a single moment. There was no direction left to run but into the mountain. And run he did, terrified of what might lie ahead, terrified of what certainly lay behind. Again and again he tried to stop, even though the voices were growing louder behind him, but found that he couldn't. He kept rolling and tumbling and tripping forward, pulled by a force he couldn't see. And then he stumbled and fell onto a bed of flowing hair, and lifted his torch toward the black emptiness, and gazed up into a face.

Long ago, while visiting a distant cousin, Worvil had accidentally taken a wrong turn and ended up opening the door of someone else's cottage. He had walked in upon a beautiful woman sitting on the edge of a bed and bending down to kiss her child good night—a tender, private moment, interrupted by his mistake. He had felt warmed by the sight, and ashamed because he had no right to see it. Strangely, that was his first thought as he lay there in the giant's cave: *I'm so sorry to intrude. You deserve to be here. I don't.*

He had expected, as anyone might, that a giant would be monstrous. But in fact, it seemed to him that everything about the giant was exactly the right size and shape, and that he, Worvil, was abnormally small. He felt as if he were looking at the only real man in the world. That was a real eye, a real nose, a real mouth. His own were merely tiny shadows.

Inside of Worvil a battle was waging—a battle

between smallness and bigness, between shrinking and growing. Part of him, the part that had been shrinking for years, wanted to turn and run in the opposite direction. And the other part, a new, unfamiliar, slowly growing part, wanted to kneel and take one of the giant coils of hair in his hands and kiss it. He lay still, and stared, and forgot the wild beating of his heart.

But a few moments later, the spell of awe that held Worvil was broken by new sounds—the rumbling of footsteps and voices behind him. As softly and as quickly as he could, he went back the way he'd come to block the intruders from coming in.

"Get out of the way, coward! Where's my daughter? Persimmony! My darling Persimmony!" Mrs. Smudge swept by him with a little shove, followed closely by Flack, who carried a torch, and Ned, who carried the last remaining sack of pepper. Behind them were half a dozen other pepper mill workers, their angry stomps echoing in the tomb-like space as they ran toward what they thought was a hoard of gold.

Worvil was beside himself. "Shhhh! Shhhhhhhhh! Don't say a word! Go back! You don't understand!" But his warnings went unheeded. The rebels marched straight into the large cavern—

—and stopped.

Slowly, silently, Flack fell backward unconscious. The torch knocked against the stone wall, and the flame went out.

Mrs. Smudge's mouth opened wider and wider. Worvil saw the breath building in her chest and knew that if he did not do something it would spill out into an ear-splitting scream, and then they would all be a giant's breakfast. He sprang to her side and clamped his hand tightly over her mouth, smothering the scream just as it reached her lips.

Worvil's sudden movement, unfortunately, caused Ned to snap. He jumped a foot into the air, threw his hands up in panic, and fled back into the tunnel. And suddenly there was a single sack of pepper flying through the air.

The sack flew   up
                    up
               up
          up
nearly disappeared into the blackness above their heads
p   a   u   s   e   d
then began its descent.

Eight people (the ninth was still lying unconscious) lunged forward at one time. Eight pairs of legs tangled themselves up in one knot, sending

everyone into a heap on the cold cave floor. Eight pairs of arms fought their way through the human pile to catch the falling sack. Someone's elbow went into someone else's eye. Worvil felt a knee pressing against his ribs. His torch rolled out of reach and lay still burning in a pile of stones.

Worvil saw the entire Future stretched out before him. He imagined the burst of pepper from the sack as it hit the floor. The snorting and sputtering and sneezing of an angry giant aroused from his long sleep. The exploding mountain. The boulders crushing them all to bits. The castle lifted up high and then dashed into the sea. The gigantic feet treading the villages into pancakes. The leveled trees. The ruined farmlands. Persimmony—dear, kind Persimmony—

But then, with a soft, harmless *thump*, the sack of pepper landed squarely on Mrs. Smudge's stomach.

For one brief moment, the mound of people stopped wriggling and heaved a sigh of relief. In the next moment, they were all untangling themselves and hastily heading for the exit—desperately straining to run forward as the giant's inhaling kept sucking them back again. Mrs. Smudge, carrying the sack as gingerly as if it were a baby, was the first to vanish into the pitch-black tunnel that led to the sunlit, outdoor, giant-less world. Two of the pepper mill workers grabbed the unconscious Flack by his feet and dragged him along behind them.

Worvil was trampled and flung to the side by those trying to escape. He tried to catch his balance but tripped in the coils of the giant's hair and rolled over and over until he was wrapped in the thick, tangled strands. When he stopped rolling, the others had gone. But behind him, within inches of his back, he could sense the nearness of the giant's wrinkled cheek. The hairs on his neck stood on end. He didn't dare turn around to look. He didn't dare move a muscle. He stared at his torch, lying far out of reach, and lay huddled in the bed of hair, silent and alone.

No, not alone—there was the unseen Sleeper beside him. There was the Snore. But Worvil didn't mind the sound anymore, for he knew that as long as he heard it, the giant was still asleep. And as bad as a sleeping giant is, it is not the worst possibility.

Chapter 20

IN WHICH CAPTAIN GIDDING SHOWS HIS VALOR WITH POETRY

*P*ersimmony *admitted later that* slathering sticky tree sap all over one's hair and body and clothes and then rolling in leaves so that one is completely covered is not the most comfortable sort of disguise. But it was the best disguise she could think of for invading the Leafeater city. The soldiers had been appalled that their uniforms were going to be ruined. Captain Gidding had gallantly offered to be covered with the pine needles, which no one else wanted, and he looked as prickly as a pincushion as the two of them passed through an arch into a seemingly endless corridor with doors lining either side.

At last they came to a place where two corridors intersected, and Persimmony stopped. Captain Gidding, however, kept right on walking. "I climbed a hill as high as hope," he was murmuring to himself. "Hope . . . mope, trope, grope, . . .

"Captain Gidding," said Persimmony. "CAPTAIN GIDDING!"

"Hm? Oh! I'm so sorry," the captain said, turning around and coming back to where Persimmony stood. "I simply can't figure out the next line of my poem."

"We're at a crossing. Are we going to go left, right, or straight?"

"Oh!" The captain looked around, puzzled. "Well, I don't suppose it really matters, since we have no idea where any of them lead. If you ask me, I've always preferred *right* myself, since it isn't *wrong*, and I hate being *left* behind, and straight ahead just seems too obvious, and you know good poems are never obvious."

"We're not in a poem, Captain Gidding, we're in a city. And we're also in a hurry."

"Patience, patience! You can't rush art."

"Okay," sighed Persimmony. "Right, then." She dropped a few leaves as she walked so they could find their way back—hoping the leaves would not be eaten in the meantime.

They made their way down another identical lamp-lit corridor, until at last they came to a dead end. All around them were wooden doors. Persimmony opened one and walked in.

It was a small, humble dwelling with four beds. At one end of the room there was a flat slab of stone balanced on top of a large rock, forming a table, and a large sign hanging on the wall over the table:

Please observe the following rules in accordance with the Code of Courtesy:

If you can't say anything with your mouth shut while you're eating, don't say anything at all.

If you *must* bite your nails, bite them behind your back.

Whatever you do, don't yawn.

The walls were painted here just as they had been in the meeting hall, with twisted vines running along the edges and over the doorways, and colorful scenes on all sides. "Exquisite," said Captain Gidding. "That pattern of painted vines above the doorway looks just like a fish caught in a net.

Amazing! It makes me feel positively poetic. I think another verse is coming."

Persimmony appreciated Captain Gidding's willingness to go to the depths of the earth to help her in her quest, but he had a very bad habit of getting distracted by other things along the way. A fish caught in a net? How was a fish supposed to help them?

"That's wonderful, Captain Gidding, but maybe the poem would come more quickly if we were walking." She opened one of the doors and walked into the next room.

The captain lingered behind. "I climbed a hill as high as hope," he was murmuring again. "What else rhymes with hope?"

"*I washed my mouth out with some soap,*" offered Persimmony, hoping that if she played along, he would follow her more closely.

It worked. "That's a good try!" he exclaimed, coming quickly to her side as she chose another door into another empty chamber. "Unexpected! But not exactly the *meaning* I was after. Perhaps another line in between will help . . .

I climbed a hill as high as hope;
I swam a sea as deep as dread . . ."

The next door led into another long corridor, and Persimmony walked more quickly. "I stole three pounds of cantaloupe and hid them all under my bed!" she shouted over her shoulder.

Captain Gidding rushed to keep up. "Creative, but not quite the right *moral* message, you know. Perhaps—"

"Shh!" Persimmony whispered suddenly. There was a rumbling of footsteps behind them. She beckoned to the captain. "Crouch down against the wall and pretend you're a pile of leaves." They did so, and a few seconds later two Leafeaters walked down the corridor. The man carried a shovel over his shoulder and wore a hat made entirely of dandelions tied together in knots. The woman had a thick grass skirt that fanned out as wide as she was tall. On her head was an impossibly high mound of braided, root-like hair. Behind them, marching solemnly two by two, was a group of about twenty more Leafeater men carrying their own shovels.

And then, just as they passed by Persimmony and Captain Gidding, the man in the dandelion hat accidentally stepped on the edge of the woman's skirt. It ripped right off, revealing a pair of long, brightly colored underwear.

Tossing his shovel away, the Leafeater man lunged to save the skirt and grabbed the woman instead, landing on top of her on the ground. The tower of hair fell off her head and rolled away.

Persimmony had to press both hands over her mouth to hold in the laughter. But to her amazement, she was apparently the only person to have found the event funny. Two Leafeaters quickly stepped up behind the unlucky couple and helped them to their feet, handing the shovel back to the man and returning the woman's skirt and wig to their proper places. All stood in respectful silence until their ruffled leader composed himself and said in a loud, deep voice: "My fellows, just now I was guilty of breaking the First Rule of the Code of Courtesy: 'In all things be dignified.' And for this I am most truly and humbly sorry."

"*We forgive you,*" replied the others solemnly. And without further ado, the group turned and proceeded through a doorway in the corridor as if nothing had happened.

The last four Leafeaters were just about to pass through the door when Persimmony heard a rustling beside her, and Captain Gidding's voice cried out, "I've got it! . . .

I climbed a hill as high as hope;
I swam a sea as deep as dread;
I bound my fear up with a rope
To hear what Weeping Willow said."

Persimmony cringed and held her breath. The last Leafeaters stopped, turned, and looked in their direction.

"That pile of pine needles is producing very bad poetry," said one.

"The more upsetting thing, my friend," said another, "is that a pile of pine needles is producing poetry at all. It's ruining my appetite." He pulled the pine needles out of Captain Gidding's beard and gasped. "A Sunspitter!"

"Two Sunspitters!" said a third Leafeater, yanking Persimmony to her feet.

"But how did they find their way down into the city? It is a thing unheard of since the secret entrances were devised three hundred years ago. A Sunspitter underground? Why, it's preposterous—revolting! You know what the great poet Rhufus Rhododendron once wrote:

And lo! when I go among such ill-mannered creatures I feel like I am swimming in cold, slimy, slippery goo up to my neck,
And all that I can say is BLECK."

Captain Gidding stood up straight and drew his sword out of its sheath with an impressive flourish.

"We are here on an urgent mission from King Lucas the Loftier."

Immediately three shovels were pointed straight at him, and Persimmony felt something sharp pressing against her shoulder blades. "Please believe that under normal circumstances I would never harm a girl," said the Leafeater standing behind her, "but if you don't put away your sword I shall be forced to run my pickax through her insides."

Captain Gidding put away his sword.

"Quick, you must help us," Persimmony said in a rush. "We've got to find the rest of the shovels, I mean the diggers, and make them stop tickling the giant— I mean, digging into the mountain, because you see, you only *think* it's a mountain, but it's really a giant that looks like a mountain—because it's covered up with dirt, of course—and so there really is no gold for you to find. Well, there *is* gold, but the gold is really a belt buckle, and if you tried to dig all the way to the belt buckle you'd hit his feet first—at the edge of the mountain, which is where you are at the moment. Or at least, the other Leafeaters who are digging are there, because of course you are here, and so you absolutely *must* help us find them as quickly as possible so we can save the kingdom from getting squashed. Do you understand?" That had not quite come out the way she intended.

The Leafeaters stared at her and then at one another.

"Tragic," said one, "to see the complete breakdown of sanity in such a young girl. But no more than one would expect from a Sunspitter. Who wouldn't go mad living among such people?"

"I can assure you," cried Captain Gidding, "my noble companion is not mad. She is brave and honest, and has the hair to prove it!"

"She has very dishonest-looking hair, if you ask me," said the Leafeater with the pickax, gazing at her head critically and ignoring the belt she held out for inspection.

"But one of your own people, Rheuben Rhinkle, believed me," Persimmony insisted, "when I saw him in Candlenut yesterday. He is the one who told me how to find the entrance to Willowroot."

"Aha, Rheuben Rhinkle! He's a very good artist, you know, but not quite right in the mind."

"The question is, what to do with these two?"

"Let's tie them up and take them to one of the store-rooms until Chief Rhule decides what to do with them."

"But we only have one rope."

The first speaker looked back at Persimmony and the captain. "Which one of you is more important?"

"I am," said Captain Gidding immediately. "She's not important at all."

Persimmony looked at him in surprise, for it was so unlike him to say such a thing. Then she saw him wink at her. "That's right," she said slowly. "I'm not important. I just came along to—to carry the provisions." She held up her basket to show them.

"I never can tell these Sunspitters apart," the Leafeater sighed. "They all look the same to me. But since that one has a sword, he's obviously more dangerous. This little one surely can't do much harm. She is only a child, after all. Perhaps she could be healed of her Sunspitterness. We could give her a drink of our—"

"No, no!" said another. "At least not yet. You know what the taste of *that* will do to one of *them*. And Chief Rhule will surely want them to be able to talk and answer questions."

As the Leafeaters said these things, one of them unwound a rope from around his waist and approached Captain Gidding. The captain jumped and wiggled and thrashed about (all the while winking frantically at Persimmony), so that it took all four of the Leafeaters to hold him down and bind him up. Persimmony didn't waste a moment. But instead of going back the way she and the captain had come, she dashed through the doorway where the dandelion man and the wigged woman had gone. Without daring to look behind her or slow down, she ran through another door, and then another.

Can't do much harm! Only a child! She could be dangerous if she wanted to be.

She would do this alone. There would be only her, and the giant's hair, and that would have to be enough. *I've got to practice what I'm going to say this time,* she thought as she ran down another corridor. And so she yelled, "STOP, IN THE NAME OF THE KING!" as severely as she could.

Perhaps that was too strong. They might not respond well to a direct order from a strange young girl. She tried again in a more persuasive tone of voice, "Stop, if you please, in the name of the king."

And then with more emphasis—"*Stop, in the name of the king.*"

And then in a pleading manner—"Will you be so kind as to stop in the name of the king?"

How silly of me, she thought. *Why would they stop in the name of the king anyway? They're angry at the king.* She said softly, "Stop!" and then loudly, "Stop!" and then sobbingly, "Sto-ho-ho-hop!"

And then, as she opened the door at the end of the corridor and rushed into the room beyond, Persimmony tripped over a shovel and stopped.

Chapter 21

In Which King Lucas and Worvil Have Too Little Lunch, and Persimmony Has Too Much

King Lucas was having trouble finishing his bowl of sweet potato soup. It just wasn't the same without pepper, but he didn't think he could stomach the slightest pinch of pepper that day, or any day for a very long time.

This was worse than discumbersomebubblating. This was worse than the worst word he could think of. This was distressinglydismallydolorouslydisastrouslycalamitouslyagonizinglylamentablyirredeemablyinsupportablynightmarishly bad.

Half a dozen clay pots sat before him on the table. He had forced the potter to give him every pot that the soldiers had brought up, in the hope that something better than milk might come out. Maybe not pepper, not right now, but something more worthy of a king. Theodore had shaken his head sadly and warned the king that he would probably not like the contents.

The potter was right. Out of these pots had come a toothbrush, a pair of brown stockings, a fishing rod, an invitation to the annual Candlenut autumn festival, a dozen turnips, and a book that reeked of dust.

Not only that, but all of his servants kept disappearing from the castle, and Lucas knew it was the potter's fault. Everywhere he looked, it seemed, he spotted Theodore's wretched cane tapping and his wrinkled face bent over in whispered conversation with someone. He thought he heard words like "dangerous" and "leave immediately." And the next thing he knew, his favorite back-scratcher had gone to visit a sister on the Northern Shore, and his pastry chef had vanished in the middle of the night, called away (supposedly) by some emergency in Bristle-bend involving a cream puff. And even those who were still there kept jumping at the slightest noise and peering around corners fearfully, as if they expected something or someone to burst through a tapestry and eat them.

"They are all against me, every one of them," he said. "I'm surrounded by traitors."

And then, with sorrow tickling his throat as he re-membered the pepper—"Do they hate me *that much*?"

He laid his head in his arms. The tough outer rind had begun to peel away from his soul, and the sight underneath was not a pleasant one.

Something soft brushed against the side of his leg. He lifted his head. It was the cat from the tower—the barely-skin-and-bones stray creature to whom he had defiantly given the milk from Theodore's pot. It was a little less skin-and-bones now, and it rubbed against Lucas's foot and purred. The cat was gazing up at him with an expression on its face he could not quite make out, and there was a good reason for this: The king had never in his life seen such an expression, or worn one either. It was the look of gratitude. But though he had no name for it, he liked it.

"I don't suppose you like sweet potato soup?" he asked. "It's a little cold . . ." In answer, the cat leaped gracefully onto his lap. Lucas pulled the bowl of soup closer to the edge of the table and let the cat drink it right down to the last drop.

The little body was warm and trusting, and now that Lucas looked closely he could see that the gray hair was spotted with black specks. "Like pepper," he said aloud. "At first all I wanted was pepper, and now I can't seem to get away from it. That's what I shall call you: Pepper." He sighed a deep, grand, lofty, slightly quivering sigh and stroked the cat's head gently. "It's you and me against them all, Pepper. There's nobody in the world more miserable than we are."

Lucas was not quite correct.

No one came to rescue Worvil. The hours leaked by, but he was too frightened to move. Had the Rumblebumps abandoned their Grand Stomper so soon? He might have expected it. They were silly, unfaithful, and, most infuriating of all, utterly incapable of seeing the negative side of any situation.

Then something happened. It happened so quietly and unexpectedly that Worvil hardly even knew it had happened until, in the middle of a particularly long daydream about lying in his own bed in his house atop the mangrove tree, he realized that the Snore had stopped.

For a few moments there was absolute silence, and it gave Worvil the feeling that the whole world had disappeared. In fact, he wished very much that it *had* disappeared, because the only other possibility he could think of was that the giant had awakened and this was the calm before the storm that would be the destruction of everything.

But then, just as quietly as the Ceasing of the Snore, a new thing happened. The giant started to exhale. A tremendous rush of air surged through the cavern, lifted Worvil right off his feet, and tossed him like a leaf caught in a strong wind. He twisted and tumbled in the net of the giant's hair, getting more tangled than ever, until the giant's breath finally settled into a steady river of warmth.

It was noon. Mount Majestic stopped rising and began to fall.

After tripping over the shovel, Persimmony had rolled to a stop in a large room full of the biggest kettles she had ever seen in her life. A Leafeater stood at each one stirring the contents with a long wooden spoon, and others were shaking little jars of spices and throwing in acorns and seeds. The air was filled with the overpowering smell of wet leaves and paprika. Towers of leaves hid the walls around the edges of the room. Another Leafeater with a huge, wide shovel was scooping them up and dropping them into various kettles.

Persimmony crouched among the leaves, hoping her own disguise was still intact and that no one would notice her until she could sneak out of the room. Apparently she blended in perfectly, for the Leafeater with the shovel came to her side of the room next, and before she could wriggle away she was being shoveled up, swung through the air, and dropped into a kettle of stew.

Luckily, the stew was cold.

Unluckily, Persimmony's mouth was open in sur-

prise as she fell, and she took a big gulp of the salty, earth-tasting liquid before she could turn herself right side up again and come to the surface, choking and gasping for air.

The Leafeater woman standing over her screamed and whacked her on the side of the head with the wooden spoon. Persimmony scrambled out of the kettle onto the floor, clasping her drowning hat onto her dripping hair and trying to spit the bitter taste out of her mouth. A dozen pairs of bony feet stomped on her as if she were a cockroach scuttling across the kitchen.

"A Sunspitter!"

"How unsanitary!"

"In our stew! How rude!"

The Leafeaters furiously salted and spiced her as she held up her soggy, leafy skirt and ran out the door—and through another door, and through another (how many doors could one city have?) until she spotted a wooden cupboard in a corner, climbed inside, and caught her breath. Only then did she realize that she had left her father's basket floating in the kettle, and that a little pine-needle grasshopper and turtle would soon become someone's lunch.

She was too tired to cry. She felt the sorrow bubbling up like a boiling pot of soup, but it stayed inside of her and burned her heart.

Chapter 22

In Which the King Is Left Alone, and Everything Is Turned Upside Down

*K*ing *Lucas was sitting* sideways on the throne, his legs thrown over the armrest, his crown hanging over one eye, and a gray cat sleeping on his lap.

The old steward approached nervously. "Your Highness, everyone is leaving the castle. Your Highness?" Behind him were the professor, the archaeologist, the potter, and the royal musician holding the Lyre.

"Yes, I heard you," said Lucas curtly.

The steward shifted from one foot to the other. "That is, *if* it is okay with you."

Lucas carefully put Pepper on the floor, then bounded from his throne in a tantrum and approached the trembling steward. "Of course it isn't okay with me! Who will cook my meals? Who will bring me my slippers and dust my crown and scratch my back and announce my visitors? No one! Why? Because of a lot of silly rumors that no one should have heard in the first place. *Nothing is going to happen* . . . and even if something were to happen, *which it won't,* I can't see how leaving me alone here will do you any good. The Future will come whether you like it or not."

"Yes, that is true, that is true. But you see, if the giant wakes up while we're down in the villages, we *might* be killed. But if the giant wakes up while we're on top of the mountain, we will *definitely* be killed. And we much prefer *might* over *definitely.* So we're leaving . . . um, with Your Highness' permission, of course."

"Why do you need my permission? No one needed my permission to barge into my bathroom and pour pepper into my tub. No one needed my permission to dig a tunnel through the middle of my mountain to find my gold. Go! Go, hide your head under a bucket somewhere. Don't worry about me!"

The archeologist bowed low to the ground. "Nothing is *further* from our purpose than to appear *disloyal* or to go against Your Highness' *personal wishes,* but under the circumstances it seems most *safe, sensible,* and *expedient*—that is, it would most *behoove* all concerned—to come to the point—"

"Why start now?" Lucas muttered.

" —for us to get to lower ground immediately."

"Your Highness," Professor Quibble cut in.

"Don't tell me," interrupted Lucas. "You're leaving too."

The professor bent his leg upward, placed his fingers on the bridge of his nose, raised his arm gracefully, and screwed his face into an especially wise expression—then he let his arm and leg fall again and shrugged his shoulders. "Yes," he said. "Do you think, with all the servants leaving and the castle nearly empty, the peasants will not seize upon this opportunity to storm the place and take it for themselves? The castle guard has not returned—except for a few soldiers too wounded to be of any help. *I* am certainly not foolish enough to stay here unprotected."

Lucas kicked his leg against the side of the throne and shoved his crown out of his face. "Persnickety was supposed to come back and tell us if she saw a giant in the Snoring Cave, and she didn't. So there! No giant. And by the way, whatever happened to Badly?"

"Your servant Badly has returned from the Western Shore with a worse cold than before," said the potter. "He says he saw a crowd of people running out of one of the caves and screaming about seeing the head of a giant. He doesn't know what happened to the Rumblebumps . . . or Worvil." The potter paused, and a worried expression crossed his face. "Persimmony Smudge has disappeared."

"*Smudge?* Her name is Smudge?"

"Of course. Badly announced it when we arrived."

"No he didn't. I distinctly heard him say SssM-MMMnnggggPHPHPH." Lucas smacked his forehead. "It must run in the family."

"What do you mean?" asked the potter, startled.

"Well, according to *my* father's journal, some crazy man named Smudge came to him a long time ago and said he saw a giant's head in a cave, and my father sure let him know what was what and who was who! And now we go and let his *daughter*—I suppose that's what she is—go to the same cave! And she disappears too! It figures. No respect for the king."

The sky broke open in Theodore's face. He stared down at his cane, nodding his head and mumbling, "Simeon Smudge saw the giant? So that was it. Aha. Yes. It's all clear now." Then he directed a piercing gaze at the king. "Your Highness, your father was a very foolish man to send away Simeon Smudge, and unfortunately he will never know all the consequences of his actions. I think that this kingdom will someday be very thankful that Persimmony is just like her father. I hope that you will not be like yours."

Lucas looked at the potter as if the wrinkled hand holding the wooden cane had just slapped him across the face. "How dare you? No one is leaving! I'll bar the castle gates, I'll tie your shoelaces together so you trip, I'll hide your trunks where you'll never find them . . ."

"Why don't we see what the Lyre-That-Never-Lies has to say," suggested Theodore.

The royal musician came forward and strummed the beautiful instrument softly. The words that came out were tight and high-pitched, as if the heart of the Lyre were stretched nearly to the point of breaking.

Beware of lofty places
When a mountain has two faces.
If you do not heed my warning,
All your joy will turn to mourning.

The music rang coldly in the throne room and faded away in an instant.

"Well, that doesn't help one bit!" cried Lucas. "Which morning? Tomorrow morning?"

"I think it meant 'mourning' as in crying," said Professor Quibble.

"Of course it did. I always cry in the morning. There is nothing worse than getting out of bed. And whoever heard of a mountain having two faces?"

"This one does," said Theodore. "The face the world sees from the outside and the one that lies hidden on the inside."

"I don't believe it," said Lucas.

"Will you ignore the Lyre's warning then?" Theodore shook his head and tapped his cane on the floor.

Lucas was silent for a long time. His head hurt from all this thinking. His motto had always been "Eat first, think later," and somehow he usually never managed to get around to the second part. "If *you* had done your job and made us a pot with something *useful* in it," he said, "instead of feathers and flutes, this whole problem could have been solved by now."

"For the last time, I am not the one who puts gifts in the pots!"

"Well, if you don't, who does?"

"I have no idea," said the potter. "Who puts words of truth into the strings of a Lyre? Perhaps there are some things that we are not meant to understand. Without a few mysteries and a few giants, life would be a very small thing, after all."

"I'm not leaving," Lucas said firmly. "Even if

there is a giant, *which there is not*, how will I ever hold my head up high again if I give in now? Shall I disgrace the memory of my father by running away from my throne at the first sign of danger? No! Life is full of dangers. Why, just the other day, I burned my tongue while drinking my tea. Is that any reason for throwing out the teakettle? This has been the home of the kings and queens of the Island at the Center of Everything for hundreds of years, and I'll be flibbertigibbeted—"

"Excuse me, Your Highness, but there's no such word as 'flibbertigibbeted,'" Professor Quibble interrupted.

"Well, there is now! I'll be flibbertigibbeted if I stoop to the level of those who'd rather be crushed under a giant's foot than thrown into the sky by an exploding belt buckle!"

Lucas stopped to catch his breath, hoping his speech had sounded brave and noble enough to convince his listeners. But the truth was that King Lucas the Loftier had never gone down from the mountain in his entire life. It meant no longer being On Top of Majestic, no longer being Lofty. It meant descending into the world of Everybody Else. He would have no idea what to do, where to go, how to behave. He wouldn't know who he was anymore.

In the end, everyone did leave the castle. Everyone except the king. Lucas stood alone in the silence of the empty castle and listened to the rumble of footsteps and the rattle of wheels fade away. Then he began climbing the stairs of the highest tower.

After a few steps he felt a familiar, soft body nudging his feet. It was the gray cat.

"Go, Pepper," he said with a stone weighing down his heart. "Everyone else has gone. Go and catch up with them." But the cat stood still and stared up at the king lovingly.

Lucas's heart rose a fraction of an inch. "Aha! So there is still one loyal subject left in my land. Come along then, Pepper, and we shall look down upon those cowards together. Giant, my foot!"

He went halfway up the staircase and stopped. "Wait. No, Pepper. You can't come with me. I don't believe there's a giant. I don't believe anything's going to happen to the mountain or the castle. But still, it is *possible.* There is a tiny, tiny, tiny, tiny chance that I *might* be wrong. And *if* I'm wrong, and there is a giant, and the giant wakes up, then it would be a very bad thing for you to be in the tower with me. Go on down, you silly cat. Go and find a safer home."

And he turned again and walked the rest of the

way up the stairs, but when he reached the tower the cat was still with him, close at his heel. Its purring was the only sound in the entire castle. Just inside the door of the tower room sat the pot Theodore had made for him, once full of milk, now empty.

Beware of lofty places . . .

Lucas sat down on the top step, picked up the cat, and held his face against its warm fur.

"Oh, Pepper, what shall I do?"

News spreads quickly on an island, and the bigger the news the more quickly it spreads. A barefoot basket maker's daughter telling stories of a giant sleeping underneath the mountain was one thing. But it was hard to argue with nine shivering, horrified, bloodshot-eyed, respectable citizens who all swore up and down that they had stood nose to nose with, well, a Gigantic Nose. Not to mention a Tidal Wave of Hideous Eyebrows. Hysteria hovered over rooftops like a storm cloud about to burst, terror whispered in the back of broom closets, and there was a general epidemic of fainting fits.

Flack organized a campaign to protest the giant's existence and posted notices all over the town of Candlenut: "Justice for the normal people! No creatures over twenty feet tall will be tolerated in the kingdom!" All members of the Citizens Against Giants vowed to turn their backs to Mount Majestic until their grievances were resolved.

The sweet potato farmer who had once scoffed at Persimmony's announcement put a cooking pot on his head, wore a sign around his neck that said, "IT'S THE END OF THE WORLD, TOOTE-LOO, TOOTELOO!" and roamed the town yelling, "Listen to me, all you reckless souls who think you will live forever, for the world is a bottomless bowl turned inside out and the radishes will be made into mud pies and the banana trees will sprout pickles and the sky will rain oysters and two plus two will be seventeen forevermore! Woe, woe, woe to us who live to see this day!"

Those who stopped to listen were met by Jim-Jo Pumpernickel selling his Super-Deluxe Extra-Resistant Giant-Proof Helmets.

It certainly did not help matters when all of the servants and residents of the castle (except the king) swarmed down the mountain with trunks of all their possessions, carts of wounded soldiers, and rumors of battles and belt buckles. For hours the streets were haunted by the specter of a white-haired potter, hunched with age and worry, begging everyone to find a place of safety underground or out of sight, and asking if anyone had seen a little girl with mouse-colored hair or a woman wearing a purple and yellow handkerchief.

Even Professor Quibble was forced to admit that the Facts were looking more and more unpleasant by the hour.

The unpleasant Facts rushed into Persimmony's head as soon as she woke up in the cupboard where she had hidden from the furious Leafeater cooks. How long had she been asleep? How did one tell time in this underground city? *What if it's already over?* she thought frantically. *What if I've slept through everything? What if the giant is up there walking around on the earth, and I'm the one who will be trapped underground forever? What if Mount Majestic has crumbled to pieces, and everyone is dead except me?*

And then she was ashamed of herself. She was acting just like Worvil. She climbed out of the cupboard and wondered what to do next.

This room was exactly like every other room she had run through—the same leaves, the same spare furniture, the same beautifully painted walls. She was lost. She had no idea where the captain or the soldiers were. She had no idea where the Leafeater with the dandelion hat had gone. She needed a new perspective. She needed to see things from a different point of view. Her fingers and toes itched to move, but the mockery of the hat maker in Candlenut still rang in her ears. Well, no one was here now to make fun of her. She sighed, turned over, and stood on her head.

The situation didn't look any better upside down, but it did look a lot more interesting. The beds seemed much more comfortable. She imagined what the Leafeaters' lives would be like if they occasionally read their rules of courtesy from this angle:

Whatever you do, don't yawn.

If you *must* bite your nails, bite them behind your back.

If you can't say anything with your mouth shut while you're eating, don't say anything at all.

CODE OF COURTESY:
RULES IN ACCORDANCE WITH THE
PLEASE OBSERVE THE FOLLOWING

She found herself face-to-face, so to speak, with the painted vines that ran along the bottom of the wall near the floor—hiding behind a bed or a chest or a chair, racing around the room, peeking into and out of corners, and then rushing up, up, over the frame of the door into a glorious tangle at the top. And then she saw it: a fish in a net.

Persimmony lowered her feet to the ground and stood up straight. She stepped closer. In the center of the pattern of painted vines over the door was an oval, with one end narrowing to a point and the other end narrowing and then flaring out again into two longer points—a fish. Underneath, the vines wove over and under and over and under each other like a basket—or a net. There it was, exactly as Captain Gidding had said: a fish in a net. Now that she saw the shape amidst the chaos, it was obvious. How could she have missed it before?

She turned around and stood under another doorway on the opposite side of the room. The arch of vines here was much more complicated to unravel. There seemed to be thick bundles of vines growing straight up, with thinner vines climbing up and around them. Growing out of the thinner vines were shapes that looked like leaves—yes, these were definitely leaves—and something else. Long drooping spikes covered with little round circles, like berries. No—like ripe peppercorns, ready to be picked and dried and ground into fine black pepper.

Puzzling over it in her head, she opened the door and passed into a chamber much like the one she had just left. Across from her as she entered was another door with pepper plants above it. She turned back to look at the door through which she had just come. There was the fish and the net.

So the Leafeaters painted fish and pepper plants above their doorways. What did it mean?

But this room also had a third door on the wall in between the other two, to the right of the fish door and to the left of the pepper door. Here Persimmony stood for a much longer time, her eyes following the path of the vines over and over again but finding no pattern. Only swirls. Vines swirling in circles and melting away into tiny ripples. Great rolling bodies of green, at the very edge exploding into chaos.

Smooth, billowing curves.

Rolling and crashing.

The sea.

The sea! Very slowly she turned around where she stood. Fish in nets. Ocean waves. Pepper plants. The fourth wall was blank.

This time she went through the door with the

waves above it. The door opened onto a long corridor. Directly across the corridor was another door. When she opened it and burst into this new chamber, she hardly needed to look around her to know what would be above the three doors she saw first. Straight ahead, more waves. To the right, leafy stalks. To the left, a fish in a net. She turned and looked above the door she had just entered.

There it was: the gentle shape of the mountain, and rising from its top the many spires of the castle.

Four doors. Four directions. The fishermen with their nets to the north. The billows of the sea to the east. The pepper plants to the south. And to the west—Mount Majestic.

Now she knew what to do.

Chapter 23

IN WHICH PERSIMMONY'S TALENTS ARE APPRECIATED, THOUGH NOT THE RIGHT ONES

Even knowing which way was west, Persimmony found it harder than she had hoped to discover the precise path the Leafeaters had taken. The corridors twisted, forked, doubled back on themselves, and dead-ended. Sometimes she would take a west-facing door only to end up in a corridor that turned a corner and led her east again. Her thoughts were twisting and turning too. What if (oh, there was Worvil again!) . . . what if she got so lost in this maze of tunnels that no one ever found her again? If no one knows where you are, do you still exist? If her father could vanish the way he did, what would happen to her?

But she kept choosing directions, and she kept running, and slowly she made her way farther and farther west. Finally, she came to a very wide corridor, almost like a main street, with torches lighting the path ahead.

Paintings filled the walls—lush, sweeping strokes of color, as if someone had been painting in a hurry—and all of the pictures were of Leafeaters digging. Persimmony began to run. Painted figures whizzed past her, and here and there an image of Mount Majestic itself, until finally they stopped abruptly. She nearly tripped over the jars of paint lying idly on the floor. This must be where Rheuben Rhinkle was working before he went to Candlenut to buy more paintbrushes, she thought.

And then she heard the sound she had been waiting for: the distant clatter of metal meeting earth and stone. Straight ahead, she could see a wriggling mass of colorless bodies.

The entire Leafeater city was there—men, women, and children—attacking the earth with the blind zeal of a common mission. Some stood on wooden platforms, working high above the heads of the rest. Others hauled away dirt in big buckets. The Leafeater with the hat of dandelions stood apart from the rest, surveying the progress and barking out commands:

"More to the left! Do not waste a moment, brave citizens of Willowroot, for your reward is close at hand!" This must be Chief Rhule, the one the Leafeaters in the corridor said would decide what to do with her and Captain Gidding. He certainly looked chief-ly.

Persimmony stared at the wall of dirt and rocks nearly hidden by the diggers. As clumps fell away

under the shovels' goading, she could see large patches of something underneath, something that was smooth and slightly pink and definitely not dirt.

"We've hit some sort of strange rock formation. Dig harder!" Rhule shouted. "Let's clear as wide a path as we can. We must be nearly at the foot of the mountain by now."

The *foot* of the mountain indeed!

Persimmony ran to where Chief Rhule stood, took a deep breath, and yelled, "STOP!"

At least, that was what she *meant* to do. But what actually happened was this: She took a deep breath. She opened her mouth to yell. And nothing came out.

She cleared her throat and tried again—and choked upon silence.

With all of the strength in her lungs she struggled to squeeze out a word, a sound, even a whisper. She squeezed and strained until her face turned red and her eyes watered. Chief Rhule turned around. "What under the earth? It is a Sunspitter! How did you find our secret entrances?" He stomped toward her, his dandelion hat quivering with indignation. "Are there more of you? Do you dare come with an army? Speak up, young lady, I can't hear you."

Theodore's words came back to her in a flash: *If you or I were to drink the Leafeaters' tears, we would be left speechless. We would not be able to say a single word.*

The stew!

"Rhiddle!" Rhule roared. "Your aid is needed."

One of the Leafeaters at the back of the crowd came running.

"Rhiddle, this insolent girl has invaded our city.

Moreover, I believe she has been sent by the king to stop our digging and sabotage our quest for justice. Moreover, she refuses to speak when she is spoken to. Arrest her at once."

Rhiddle gazed doubtfully at the dirty figure standing before him, and Persimmony felt her cheeks grow hot. She motioned with her hands, she pointed to the wall of earth and then to the bottom of her foot, she jumped high and waved her arms and shook her head, but the two Leafeaters were utterly baffled. Then she remembered the giant's hair and held the belt out toward Rhule.

"You know best, of course, my chief," said Rhiddle, "but I *think* if she were here to sabotage our quest for justice she would bring a sword, not a peace offering. And besides, a Sunspitter who *doesn't* speak is a vast improvement, don't you agree?"

"Peace offering?" Rhule took the strange bundle from Persimmony and looked thoughtfully at it for several minutes. "Perhaps she wants to join us in our honorable endeavor. Yes, there is a seriousness in her face that speaks of courage, loyalty, and resolve. Very well, the Leafeaters will not turn away from a well-meaning gift, however rudely delivered and—oddly shaped." He tied the hair belt around his waist and bowed to Persimmony. "Welcome to our city. Of course, you can never leave now that you've discovered our secret entrances, but have no doubt that you will always be treated with courtesy and that we will make every effort to ensure that you are warm, well-fed, and comfortable for the rest of your life. Hand her a shovel, Rhiddle. Oh, no, my dear," he added as Persimmony again pointed to the diggers and then to her feet frantically, "don't worry about your bare feet. None of us wear shoes here."

Persimmony tossed aside the shovel Rhiddle gave her, got down on her hands and knees, and began to draw a picture of Mount Majestic in the dirt with her finger.

"What an artistic flair she has!" Rhule exclaimed. "What surprising talent! It is a perfect depiction of a tortoise shell."

"And there is the tortoise inside, lying down," said Rhiddle. "Look, she has even taken the trouble to draw its tongue sticking out one end. A remarkable attention to detail."

"But she has given it many tongues, not just one. Look at them all, jutting out from the edge of the tortoise shell. They look just like little shovels. What a creative mind! What originality! It must be symbolic."

Persimmony wiped away the drawing with her hat and stomped on it in frustration. She felt exactly like the tortoise with its tongue cut off.

"Rhiddle!" said the chief suddenly. "Shame on us! We did not compliment her hat. Remember rule number sixty-three of the Code of Courtesy: Always compliment a lady's hat. No wonder she is so out of temper. Young mistress, your hat is lovely."

If only Captain Gidding were there to speak for her! Captain Gidding, who was so full of words. She wondered whether he had managed to get away from the four Leafeaters.

Words. How stupid of her. She could write a message. After all, she had been practicing her writing for months. But did "giant" begin with a J or a G?

There was no time to be indecisive. She went with her first guess and began scribbling in the dirt, "J . . . I . . . U . . . N . . ." But a stampede of Leafeaters carrying buckets of dug-up earth trampled the letters into meaningless scratches as they passed. Exasperated, Persimmony grabbed one of the smaller buckets and dumped the contents over its owner's head.

"The poor girl, she has gone mad!" cried Rhule. "Artists often do, alas."

It is one of life's great injustices that whenever you

want to cry, no tears will come, but whenever it is embarrassing and childish to cry, it happens whether you like it or not. In the past three days, Persimmony had been lost in the woods, soaked in a thunderstorm, chased by a poison-tongued jumping tortoise, offended by a king, snored upon by a giant, laughed at by an entire town, led on a wild-goose chase by a band of brainless soldiers, knocked out by a tree in the heat of her first battle, threatened with a pickax, forced to listen to a surprising amount of poetry, and nearly made into stew. This was the last straw.

The burning seeped into her nose and overflowed through her eyelids. *I've got to save the kingdom,* she wanted to tell them, but all that came out were sobs. Furious at herself, she pressed her palms against her eyes and jumped up and down several times to shake the crying out of her head. But she was trapped in her very own Ceremony of Tears.

Above her, the dirt fell away to reveal a wall of flesh lined with earth-filled creases. "Dig harder!" Rhule called out. With blind determination, the Leafeaters hacked away.

Chapter 24

In Which the Air Is Full of Fear, Suspicion, Blame, and Vegetables

The easiest way to forget how scared you are is to get angry at someone (it doesn't really matter whom), and so when it was time for the trial of the two Leafeaters, Rhedgrave and Rheuben Rhinkle, people from all over the island showed up. There was a large stage in the middle of Candlenut for auctions and festivals, and at the edge of this stage a pair of stocks had been set up. These were wooden frames with holes for a person's head and hands. "Why are we being put in these?" asked Rheuben as the heavy wood was lowered over his head. "This is a punishment. I thought we were on trial."

The magistrate ignored him. "Jury, are you

ready?" One the other side of the stage, the spice merchant, the dairy farmer, the seamstress, the carpenter, and the owner of the stolen rooster all nodded.

"I have a question," said Professor Quibble, stepping onto the stage. "Is it not true that, as the pepper mill workers have so loudly confirmed for us, there is a giant lying asleep underground with its head at the western end of the mountain and its feet at *your* end? And is it not true that at this very moment the Leafeaters are digging toward the very place where those giant feet lie? And is it not true that if the giant wakes up and the kingdom is trampled, the Leafeaters will have what they have always wanted—peace and quiet *without* all the rest of us around?"

A loud murmuring rippled outward. "But—but you can't possibly believe that the Leafeaters are trying to wake up the giant *on purpose*?" cried Rheuben.

"How dare you blame us for this unfortunate turn of events?" sputtered Rhedgrave. "We wouldn't have been digging into the mountain at all if *your king* hadn't stolen our trees and written such a rude letter to our chief."

"Perhaps if you let us go," Rheuben said, "we can

hurry back to Willowroot and stop the rest of the Leafeaters from digging any further. That brave daughter of Simeon Smudge has gone to do it, but I fear they may not believe her."

Theodore stood up suddenly from the cart where he had been resting. His eyes flashed with relief and new concern. "Persimmony! You've seen her? She is heading to Willowroot?"

But Rheuben's reply was interrupted by the other person Theodore had been seeking. "*Persimmony? Persimmony* has gone to find the Leafeaters?" Ever since that terrifying moment in the cave, Mrs. Smudge had been uncharacteristically quiet. Even when the pepper mill workers had raced through the villages spreading the news, she had done little more than wander in the fields and mutter to herself, "You foolish, foolish woman—why didn't you believe him?" Now she began shoving aside bystanders to escape from the throng. "Let me through, let me through! I've got to get to the woods. I'll search all night until I find her. My poor courageous lamb! So like her father!"

"Mother, don't leave me!" shrieked Prunella. She started to run too but suddenly found herself in the thin, firm arms of Theodore, who patted the girl's trembling shoulders and gripped his cane to steady both of them. He cast a concerned glance at her mother.

"Amelia," Theodore said gently, "she *is* like her father, and that's why you need to let her do what needs to be done." Mrs. Smudge stopped and turned to him with surprise and suspicion in her face. "Gentlemen," he continued, addressing the magistrate and the professor, "it is an excellent idea for you to let these two Leafeaters go back to their people and warn them of the danger. I suggest—"

"If you think," the magistrate sneered at Rheuben, "we're going to let you go and *trust* you to stop your conniving, unscrupulous people, then you have misjudged your judges. We weren't born this morning."

It is very difficult to maintain your dignity when your head and hands are sticking out of blocks of wood, but Rheuben was doing his best. "Come, come, let's try to be rational. Calm discussion, an honest facing of the facts, and a firm rejection of all unnecessary adjectives and adverbs—that's the way to get to the truth of things."

"The truth, nephew," grumbled Rhedgrave, "is that it is the lot of the Leafeaters to suffer. We have suffered patiently for centuries at the hands of Sunspitters."

"What about *us*?" Flack turned an accusing stare on the older Leafeater. "It's because the Leafeaters went underground so long ago that the tortoises have gone wild and taken over the Willow Woods!"

A cry of outrage burst from the townspeople of Candlenut.

"Let me remind you," said Rhedgrave coolly, "that it was because of your people's disdain for all tradition, beauty, and wisdom that our ancestors built the city of Willowroot to begin with."

"Let me remind *you*," one of the farmers hooted, "that you are outnumbered. We don't need you! We don't want you!" And the rest of the farmers began raising their rakes and pitchforks and inching closer to the captive Leafeaters.

"Have you all ever *cried*?" Rhedgrave snapped. "Really, truly *wept* over the world? Well, *we do*. A Leafeater's grief is so profound, so monumentally tragic, that a mere swallow of our tears can make one of you Sunspitters tongue-tied for days. Well! Maybe it's time you had something to cry about."

The potter lifted his hand to calm the people. "Please," he said, "don't allow your fear to cloud your good judgment. There have been many wrongs done, but no one is the villain here. We will solve nothing by warring with each other. There are much more important things to worry about—for one thing, we all need to find safe cover immediately."

"Of course there's a villain," said Flack. "Every story must have a villain. Every side must have an enemy."

Prunella burst into tears and buried her face in the potter's white beard. "I don't understand anything that's happened since we left home."

"There are many things to talk about, and many things to explain," said the potter, "but right now we *must* find places to hide."

At that moment an ear-splitting sound brought the arguing to a halt. It wasn't thunder, nor was it the growl of an animal or anything so safe—it was a deep, immense, sky-filling, heart-stopping CHUCKLE. Everyone except the Citizens Against Giants, who went on facing the other direction, turned their gaze toward Mount Majestic. The island was silent.

Dustin Dexterhoof had been trying to get everyone's attention for at least twenty minutes. He jumped onto the stage. "Pardon me, my *dear* fellow citizens, I believe you are overlooking the *obvious, inescapable,* and in fact quite *blatant* truth that, despite our *understandable* desires to blame other—"

"Spit it out!" the magistrate snarled.

"Don't you see? The only *real* enemy is the one who lies underneath that mountain."

As if in answer, the eastern end of the mountain seemed to ripple and buckle like the surface of water when a large fish swims underneath. Then it settled into solid green again.

"We'll kill the giant!" someone shouted.

"We can't kill *him*," said Professor Quibble. Now that he had finally admitted the existence of such a creature, he considered himself an expert. "There's no poison strong enough, no dagger big enough, no method of execution guaranteed to kill a sleeping giant before he has time to stir. Not to mention the fact that even if we did kill him, we'd be stuck with an enormous, stinky, decaying *corpse*."

"What right have we to kill him?" said Theodore. "He has done nothing wrong except exist—and sleep."

Fear was like a fierce ocean wave dashing itself against a wall, but the people held it back desperately with their hearts. And the more they held it back, the angrier they became.

"We're a good island! We don't deserve this!"

"Well, of course you deserve it," yelled the owner of the stolen rooster. "I am *ashamed* to be standing here in the Day of Wickedness. Many years ago, when the Lyre-That-Never-Lies prophesied that the turnip crop would come early, I told everyone that there was more to it than turnips. For a turnip is as despicable a vegetable as I've ever tasted, and if we were going to be cursed with an abundant turnip crop, it was a sign of approaching DOOM, that's what it was! But did anyone believe me?"

"If you have a prejudice against turnips, why don't you just say so?" demanded Flack.

The mad sweet potato farmer (*he* was mad—his *potatoes* were sweet) began banging on the side of his cooking-pot-hat with a pipe. "Woe, woe, woe is you! Woe is me! Woe is everyone! The sun has taken ill, and the sea is drowned! The earthworms are wiser than we are! There is no more tea in my sugar bowl!"

No one ever knew who threw the first tomato. It smacked Rhedgrave Rhinkle in the face. After that, the air was full of flying fruits and vegetables. Nearly everything in the Candlenut marketplace was soon pelting the stage and its occupants. Tomatoes, mangoes, oranges, bananas, plums, avocados, peaches, heads of cabbage, ears of corn, buckets full of carrot juice and raspberry jam, coconuts, pumpkin pies, coffee beans, eggs, turnips, sweet potatoes, blueberries . . .

And then the earth shivered, and the mountain roared.

Chapter 25

In Which a Feather and a Flute Prove Their Worth

A huge chunk of earth erupted from the end of the tunnel and crumbled to the ground, startling the Leafeater diggers, who stared at their own shovels in surprise.

"Hurrah!" shouted Chief Rhule. "Superb digging! Look at that mountain come down! Keep it up, keep it up!"

Persimmony watched miserably as the Leafeaters continued piercing the giant's foot and cheering at the unexpected success of their efforts amidst a shower of dirt. This was the moment in which everything depended upon her, and she had failed.

It's not my fault, she thought. *If Captain Gidding hadn't been so wrapped up in his poem . . . if the sol-*

diers hadn't been so stupid . . . if the Leafeaters had built a city that made sense and went somewhere . . . if the tortoises hadn't attacked us . . . if Theodore had told someone his suspicions sooner . . . if the king hadn't been so selfish . . . if the giant . . .

No, it's all my fault. If I hadn't stopped at the cottage . . . if I had run back to find the soldiers instead of getting more lost . . . if I hadn't taken a gulp of that stew . . . She was the wrong person to have gone on such a mission. She had let everyone down—Theodore, her mother, Prunella, Captain Gidding, Worvil, and worst of all, her father.

"Something always goes wrong," Worvil had said.

"So like a Smudge," the townspeople had said.

"She's not important at all," Captain Gidding had said. He had said it to protect her, of course, but deep down she knew that it was true. How could she have thought that she could save anyone? She wasn't *enough.* The giant was important. He was Somebody. He was powerful even when he was asleep— so powerful that a kingdom could be turned upside down because of him. Even if he slept for a thousand more years, while everyone else went on living and dying above him, he would still *matter.*

Suddenly she was filled with a great longing to be home. She wished she could hear her mother's comforting voice lecturing about the evils of soap, and see Prunella's quick fingers knitting a stocking, and know that it was just a dull, ordinary, normal day after all. She closed her eyes, but instead of seeing the cottage she was back in the cave, gazing at a majestic face—and feeling the breath of her father, who had once gazed at that face too.

Worvil was lying in the center of a whirlwind. The warm breath of the giant now burst out of his mouth in fierce gusts, and for the first time there was the deep, resonating throb of an immense Voice:

HA...HA... HAAAAAAAA....

Worvil could sense the massive face beside him beginning to stir, and the ceiling of the cave started to shift and rain down pebbles upon him.

He wanted to scream. He wanted to scream. He wanted to scream.

Screams echoed through the island as the trembling underfoot grew to a thunderous quaking. An avalanche of stones and dirt came rushing down the side of Mount Majestic.

Every day the mountain rose and fell—once. But

now its rising and falling was like the chaotic tossing of the waves on a stormy sea. Up and down, up and down the mountain bounced, and the castle shook as if it were a boat about to capsize.

"The island will break apart!" someone cried. "We will all fall into the ocean!" Men and women picked up their children and dashed for their homes, trampling flowerbeds as they ran. Out in the fields, the farmers hid in haystacks. The fishermen in the north took refuge underneath overturned boats, and the fruit pickers huddled in empty apple barrels. Those who had gathered to watch the Leafeaters' trial in Candlenut scrambled over the mess of food on the ground toward safety as fences flipped, chimneys tipped over, and merchants' goods went tumbling, bouncing, and spinning down the streets. A squawking, swirling, feathery tempest of ducks and chickens announced the end of the world.

With one violent quake, the stocks toppled off the stage and cracked open. Rheuben helped his uncle to his feet, then yelled to those nearby, "Hurry, get under the stage!" The magistrate, the jury, the professor, the archaeologist, the potter, and the king's steward followed the two Leafeaters under the stable wooden structure and clung to one another.

"The pepper mill!" Mrs. Smudge cried. "The

pepper mill is the strongest building around!" Grabbing the hands of Theodore and Prunella, she ran toward the edge of town, and the rest of the pepper mill workers tripped along behind them.

"Stand firm, Citizens Against Giants!" called Flack, planting his feet solidly in the town square and linking arms with Ned and the others who remained. "Faces to the sea! The ground may crumble, the sky may sink, the world may fall apart around us, but we shall not be moved!"

And back and forth through the panicking hordes of people rode Jim-Jo Pumpernickel on Toddle's back, throwing colanders and shouting, "Here, take a helmet. You can pay me later."

The castle was losing the battle. Up and down and side to side it went, and each time it landed, it lost a few more spires and towers. Flags tore loose from their poles and floated off into the empty wind. The many windows like a hundred eyes stared out in silence from the doomed precipice.

Finally, with a long, sad, vanquished moan, the castle crumbled. The highest tower lasted longest, holding on desperately to the sky, poised precariously on a heap of rubble, until with one last bounce it shot up high into the air and—while all those watching held their breath—fell into a cloud of dust.

And still the mountain shook. Deep cracks gouged the surface of the green slopes. Clearly, whatever was inside of Mount Majestic was not going to stay there much longer.

It was now obvious that the end of the tunnel was convulsing far beyond what an army of Leafeaters with shovels could accomplish. Torches clattered to the ground and went out, and one of the wooden platforms fell over as the earth in front of it wrinkled and jerked. Persimmony stared in alarm at a lined, leathery bulge of flesh. *Was that a toe?*

"Stay, stay a moment, my friends," called Chief Rhule as the tunnel lurched and more and more dirt rained down upon their heads. "A slight earthquake seems to be disrupting our work, but it will surely pass soon."

The Leafeaters paused in their digging and leaned on their shovels to rest.

There was no point in sitting still now. With a mighty burst of despair and determination, Worvil tore at the tangles of hair around him and scrambled away from the giant's face, tripping and rolling and pulling until he was free. He grabbed the torch and started toward the tunnel that led outside. All at once, it seemed, the quaking settled, and the roar ceased. The only sound was the giant's breathing, but this time the breathing sounded different.

Then Worvil nearly dropped the torch, because there was another light in the cave—another person with a torch beside him. He moved slightly, and the other light moved too, and he realized that it was his own torch and the faint glimmer of his own form reflected as in a mirror. But there was no mirror. There was a black hole, and a dazzling ring of blue, rimmed with white.

He turned fully toward it now and lifted his torch, and a magnificent eye stared back at him.

There must have been a second open eye farther above him too, but Worvil couldn't move, or take his own eyes away from the one. All of the wild fear inside him froze into an icy horror. The giant was awake. This was the end.

He had never in his life seen anything like the beauty and awfulness and stillness of that great eye. It blinked slowly in half wakefulness, fanning the cave with its lashes, and the wrinkles of age rippled at its corners. It wasn't at all like looking into the eye

of an animal. This was the eye of a person, whose mind took Worvil in and measured him.

There was nothing to do but wait to be crushed and swallowed. Worvil couldn't breathe. He stared into the eye's blue depths.

The shaking had stopped. The Leafeaters picked up their shovels again and began approaching the wall. "Now, friends," Chief Rhule shouted with enthusiasm. "Once more! Dig deep! Dig hard!"

It doesn't matter whose fault it is now, thought Persimmony. *I've got to stop it.*

Oh, how she wished Theodore were here! He would tell her what to do. Was he still in the castle? Had he found a safe place to hide? Then she remembered the feather from the Giving Pot. Glancing down, she spotted it protruding from the pocket of her dress. She pulled it out of the pocket slowly. It was such an ordinary little thing.

She glanced up again and saw Rhiddle, the Leafeater who had been called over to arrest her, striding solemnly toward the giant's bare toe. He was holding a pickax. With wooden resolve in his face and steady, deliberate aim, he swung his arms upward and prepared to strike.

No!

Persimmony ran to him and rubbed the white plume of the feather softly against the pale skin of his neck.

"Hoo-hoo-hoo-HOOOOOOOOOOO!" exclaimed Rhiddle, jumping as if he'd been bitten and landing flat on his back. The Leafeaters dropped their shovels and turned around with astonishment in their eyes.

Persimmony knelt closer to Rhiddle and tickled his stomach.

"Hee-hee-hee! Ha-ha-HAAAAAAAA-ha-ha! Whoooooooooo!" Rhiddle convulsed with giggling on the floor beside her, flailing his arms wildly but unable to fend off the feather.

The Leafeaters had never heard the sound of laughter coming from one of their own people. It echoed in the wide corridor, and one by one they came rushing over to see the source of this extraordinary behavior. "What is going on here?" yelled Chief Rhule, running toward the commotion. "What is the meaning of this rude, vulgar, indecorous, unseemly, ill-mannered—"

Three other Leafeaters got to Persimmony first and tried to take the feather away from her. But the feather floated above their heads, tossed this way and that by their grasping hands, until it landed in the towering, braided wig of the woman she had seen in the corridor. Persimmony squeezed through the confused crowd and jumped onto the woman's back, grabbing the feather and tickling every spot of skin she could. The woman squealed and giggled and threw out her arms. Her thick grass skirt whipped around. Her wig fell off, and Persimmony tickled the top of the bald head. Those standing by tried to pull her away, and she tickled them too. The feather escaped again, so she used her fingers instead.

"Stop laughing, this instant!" roared Chief Rhule. "Stop laughing! STOP LAUGHING!"

The feather caught him behind his left ear, and he broke into a chuckle that turned into a snicker that turned into a cackle that turned into a roar, until he was laughing so hard that his dandelion hat flew away and he was leaping above the heads of his subjects.

Then from the lamp-lit corridor at the back of the chaos of flying shovels and wriggling bodies came Captain Gidding, bristling with perseverance and pine needles, undaunted by whatever battle of strength or poetry he had faced with his two Leafeater captives. The soldiers followed, leaves toppling off them left and right. They took one look at the commotion before them and raised their swords to attack. But the captain was watching Persimmony carefully, and he held them back. "Don't fight them," he ordered after a moment. "Tickle them!"

The soldiers rushed into the crowd and did as they were told.

Something inside of the Leafeaters burst open. Their severe wooden faces cracked. Their colorless skin blushed into a rosy glow. Their mouths stretched into new shapes. And then an even more extraordinary thing happened: They began to tickle each other. The feather passed from person to person, and a mighty chorus of hilarity swelled inside the dim underground space. The roof rang with full-chested guffaws. Stopping for breath and looking around, Persimmony discovered that she was nearly the only person in the whole room who was not laughing.

She was torn between relief and amazement, but she couldn't laugh. The tunnel was no longer shaking, but what was happening aboveground? Were her mother and sister all right? Were they safe at home in the cottage, hiding in the cellar, wondering where she was? What was happening in the cave? How scared Worvil must be! She closed her eyes and imagined his face, the squashed potato face of a man whose imagination was too vast for his courage. *You're big, Worvil,* she told the frightened face in her mind. *You're big.*

The giant looked at Worvil. Worvil looked at the giant. *I am not big,* he said to himself. *I am small. I am very, very small.*

You're bigger than you think you are, said Persimmony.

Maybe he was. Maybe Persimmony was right. Maybe he had sizes all wrong. She had trusted him to watch over the giant. She wouldn't have trusted him if she didn't think he could do it, would she? Worvil patted his arms and legs—were they shrinking? Beneath the folds of his trousers, he felt the hard, thin form of the flute. Without daring to tear his eyes away from the Eye, he pulled the flute out with shaking hands. The last time he ever remembered not being afraid—before the fire and the tidal wave and all the other terrible things that had happened—was when he sat on his mother's lap while she sang a lullaby and rocked him to sleep.

To sleep. He would put the giant back to sleep!

What was that tune his mother used to sing? He was so little then, and he would press his ear against her chest and hear the song echoing inside of her as in a cave. He put the instrument to his lips and tried to take a deep breath and blow hard. No deep breath would come.

Concentrate, concentrate, concentrate! he told

himself. He held the flute tightly, gathered what little breath was left in his lungs, and let out a

s   l   o   w

steady

solid stream of air.

A soft note floated out the other end of the flute. More startled at the quiet sound than he had been the day before at the piercing screech, Worvil blew again, gently, and held his fingers over the holes on the wooden surface.

The note changed—and changed again—

Like a dove softly singing its greeting to the sun.

Like the Lyre wrapping its music around his beating heart.

But what was that? The giant's lips quivered as a new sound poured out of them. It was rich and deep. It was humming. The cave was flooded with a song, but it was not the melody Worvil had been playing on his flute. It was like no song Worvil had ever heard before. It reminded him of the Lyre, just a little. It seemed to echo in his very bones. It was a *big* song—too big for such a small island. It sounded like distant seas and suns and mountain summits. It sounded like *Beyond*.

Worvil's breath faltered for a moment, but he began to play again—gently, gently, as gently as a mother—and this time he played the notes that the giant was humming. The music from the flute and the music from the giant's lips waltzed together in the cave like the call of a seagull and the roar of the ocean. The creases around the giant's eyes softened into the faintest smile, and there was a peace in his face that was deeper than the peace of a star.

Across the island, those few who were not screaming thought they heard a strange sound on the wind— unfamiliar, unsettling, and yet beautiful. They strained to hear it, as though they were straining to reach for a hand that would pull them from the waves.

Persimmony felt it more than she heard it—a vibrating all around her, like the Lyre's strings when they were plucked, causing the castle to ring with song. *But that's silly, isn't it?* she thought. *Could the earth be singing?* She stared at the wall of tingling skin. She listened.

The giant's eyelids began to droop. The billows of gray hair rose and twisted and settled again as the giant turned his head to hear the flute better, and his humming faded. The rocks groaned under the weight of his weariness. The deep furrows in his forehead became smooth. His lashes swept the cave one last time and shivered on his cheek. His mouth opened wider, wider, wider into a tremendous final

YAWN

then shuddered and sighed and shut.

Worvil closed his eyes too. *Buried fear will fly away*, the Lyre had said. His heart was soaring. He breathed the lullaby, covering a world of fears and mountains and giants with the soothing blanket of sleep.

There was no more digging, and no more laughing. The Leafeaters lay exhausted on the ground, gasping for breath. The soldiers (their work done) were quietly straightening their collars. Persimmony and Captain Gidding sat tensely watching the giant's toe.

And watching.

And watching.

And watching.

All was still.

Chief Rhule lifted himself slowly from the ground and gazed in wonder at the grinning lumps that were his people. He glanced at Persimmony and the captain, then followed their eyes up to the strange wall.

"Well, look at that," he said. "It's a foot."

Chapter 26

IN WHICH MOURNING COMES IN THE MORNING

The sun rose on a silent, shocked kingdom. Those who emerged from their hiding places and blinked in the early light felt as if their hearts had been put in a jar, shaken into a hundred pieces, and spilled onto the ground again. Now all the pieces were out of order. The islanders looked at one another, wondering how to feel. No one dared to look at the mountain.

How could they ever go back to milking cows and baking bread and farming fields after this? What did ordinary things matter now that they knew such an extraordinary thing could happen—and might happen again?

Candlenut was bruised and battered. The worst of

the mess was in the center of the town. The battle of food had littered and splattered the main square with a slimy, gooey, sticky, slippery, mangoey, jammy, juicy, turnipy slop.

Rheuben and the magistrate emerged from underneath the stage and helped the king's steward to his feet. The steward quietly pointed, and only then did anyone turn their gaze upward toward Mount Majestic. The mountain looked like a tossed salad. All of the ingredients were still there—grass, dirt, rocks, wildflowers—but mixed and scrambled and settled again into a new mountain. To the islanders' eyes it looked less like something smooth and hilly and more like—*someone*—under a blanket. The steep, pointed slope on the eastern side—was that a knee? And the western side had rolled over a bit, creating a high cliff that resembled a gigantic shoulder. The castle was gone. There was nothing left but a pile of stones and a single flag waving crookedly in the breeze. "The king," whispered the steward, kneeling in a mound of squashed sweet potatoes.

At that moment, as quietly and gracefully as a fog moving over a field, a great company of slightly rosy faces drifted into Candlenut, serene and dignified—except for their mouths, which had a stretched appearance. The Leafeaters stopped at the edge of the crowded square and stared at the distraught townspeople. The townspeople looked wearily back at them, unable to be shocked by anything anymore. What were Leafeaters compared to a giant? What was a stolen rooster or a few broken eggs compared to a mountain roaring with life? Chief Rhule stepped toward the stage, respectfully removed his dandelion hat, and asked in a loud, polite voice, "Excuse me, but where is King Lucas the Loftier?"

As Persimmony followed the Leafeaters, Captain Gidding, and the soldiers out of Willowroot up into the sunlight, it seemed to her that the world had turned a hundred different colors she had never seen before. The island was still there. Mount Majestic was still there. The oaks and cedars were still standing, and *she* was standing among them. As she and the others brushed beside the bowing, whispering welcome of willow branches, she wanted to kiss the earthworms. As they emerged from the woods and passed her own cottage, she wanted to run inside and count the soupspoons or peel a potato. And as they marched into Candlenut, she had an irresistible urge to find a cow and milk it, just to know she could.

But instead of a cow, someone else greeted her. "Persimmony!" her mother screamed. "It's just as I thought—those dreadful Leafeaters kidnapped you! Did they hurt you? Did they—"

"Oh, Persimmony," cried Prunella, "how could you go running off like that when all I asked you to do was—"

"Do you have any idea what you have put your mother and sister through? How dare you go and—"

"It's been so horrible and my feet hurt so much and I was so scared—"

"Oh, my dear, delightful, disobedient, darling daughter! Why don't you answer me?"

Persimmony smiled and closed her eyes and felt herself being folded in giant arms and washed in enormous kisses. She was home.

Meanwhile, the Leafeaters were conferring with Rhedgrave and Rheuben, now gladly restored to their company. Centuries of wisdom and tradition had never prepared them for a situation like this. They had no "Morning-After-the-Giant-Almost-Woke-Up" Ceremony, no "We're-So-Sorry-for-Almost-Destroying-Everyone" Ceremony. In their entire Code of Courtesy there was no rule for what to say to those who have watched a mountain nearly erupt and a castle fall into dust with their king inside.

"We should have a funeral for the king," pro-

nounced Chief Rhule. Funerals, at least, were something Leafeaters did well, and they had plenty of tears stored up for the purpose. And the people in Candlenut numbly agreed. Someone set up a table on top of the stage to serve as a bier—something a coffin would be put on, if they had a coffin. But since they didn't, the steward brought out a portrait of King Lucas and placed it on the bier. The rest of the islanders gathered in their arms all of the torn flower petals from the gardens that had been trampled the night before by people running for hiding places.

Persimmony was very sorry about the king, of course, but she couldn't help feeling that the people around her were missing the point. After all, they were still alive. The giant was still asleep under the mountain. There was delicious bread to be baked and fresh coconuts to be picked and thousands of fish to be caught.

"Today," Chief Rhule said solemnly from the stage, "we mourn the death of our illustrious if somewhat misguided (but we will not speak ill of the dead) monarch, King Lucas the Loftier. Bravely refusing to flee in the day of peril, he chose the way of sacrifice, believing that he who would be a true leader of his people must be the first to fall."

Then Professor Quibble, standing next to him on the stage, closed his eyes and stretched his arms forward toward the crowd. "What is life?" he said. "What is death? What is happiness? *What*"—here he pounded his fist on the edge of the bier so hard that the king's portrait fell over and the steward had to set it aright again— "*is the square root of nine?*"

Then he bowed and the crowd clapped politely, but some of the people wept.

Chief Rhule continued, "We will now hear testimonies of the valor, generosity, nobility, and unsurpassed wisdom of our honorable, deceased liege."

A hush fell over the people, and there was a long, awkward pause. Then all of the people gathered in the square gasped. Behind Chief Rhule and Professor Quibble, a filthy, bareheaded boy with feathers stuck in his hair was climbing clumsily onto the edge of the stage. One arm was wrapped around a clay pot, and a scraggly gray cat inside was licking his chin. It was King Lucas.

He had been halfway down the mountain when the shaking began. He had only intended to deposit Pepper in a safe place and then return to the castle before anyone knew he had been silly enough to leave. But all at once the ground heaved forward, and the sky tipped inward, and he fell backward. The earth seemed to shatter around his feet. An avalanche of dirt tossed him as wildly as if he were caught in the breakers on the shore, stripping off his robe and shoes and crown. He didn't even have time to be terrified. After sending him bouncing all the way down to its foot, the mountain hurled him straight through the roof of a chicken coop and knocked him unconscious.

Now all the terror of last night seemed to be bouncing down the mountain and catching up with him. But despite the churning of his stomach, he stood tall with his chin held high. He was determined to show his kingdom that he was still King Lucas the Loftier.

"I know, I know," he said, holding up his hand. "This is the surprise you were hoping for. This is the happy ending that will make up for all of the terror. But before you cheer, or heap your flowers over me, let me speak." He gulped and took a deep breath, for he had spent a long time planning how to say this next part. "Despite all my best intentions, I *may*, in the past, sometimes, perhaps maybe occasionally, not have been *entirely* fair, and at times when I was angry—for good reason of course—at the stupid actions of other people, have said or done things that might, by some, be considered unwarrantable, or objectionable, or in-icky-table—I mean iniquickly—I mean—"

"Wrong?" offered Professor Quibble.

"If you want to put it that way," Lucas muttered. "But I know that there is so much love and generosity in this kingdom that you will have no trouble overlooking some small mistakes, and we can forget all of this ever happened and live as happily as we were before." He paused to let his words sink in.

"Well, of all the rotten, stinking, low-down, nasty tricks!" rose the shrill voice of a woman who, judging from her own strong stink, was evidently one of the fishermen's wives. Pushing her way to the front of the crowd, she jumped onto the stage and began hitting the king over the head with a broom. "Making us think you were dead"—WHACK—"watching us stand here like fools when there's so much important work to be done"—WHACK—"like putting our lives together again"—WHACK—"and calming our children"—WHACK—"and figuring out what"—WHACK—"to do"—WHACK—"next!" Lucas threw his arm up to protect himself. With one more WHACK the broom broke in half, and the magistrate finally managed to pull the woman away.

"Can't you recognize an apology when you hear one?" Lucas cried, stamping his foot. "Don't you think I've suffered too? Look at that!" He pointed behind him, toward the mountain and the ruins of his castle. "I've lost everything! All my possessions are buried! The only thing I have left in the whole wide world is *one clay pot*! I fell all the way down a mountain and got a bump on my head, I had to sleep on an itchy pile of hay, and I haven't eaten a bite of breakfast today. I think I deserve a *little* sympathy."

"Oh, leave the poor king alone," yelled Mrs. Smudge. "Better a tyrant you know than a giant you don't, that's what I always say."

The islanders were even more flummoxed than ever. Their mountain was not a mountain anymore but a sleeping giant. Their dead king was not dead anymore but standing in front of them holding a cat and smelling a bit like a barnyard. A funeral had at least given them a purpose, a way of putting to rest what had happened and postponing any decisions. Now what? For several long minutes the people stared at the king, and the king stared at the people, and the Leafeaters stared at the bier, unsure how to finish the ceremony gracefully when the deceased was no longer deceased.

And then the Rumblebumps came.

ᐒ Chapter 27 ᐐ

IN WHICH PERSIMMONY SMUDGE SWEEPS A FLOOR

They came like whispers. They came like the sad, plodding hours of the night. From the west the Rumblebumps slowly slinked into the town, barely lifting their big flat feet off the ground with each step. Their empty pockets sagged uselessly from their many coats, their chins hung so low they almost brushed the dirt, and their eyes overflowed with sorrow.

The sight of them filled Persimmony's heart with an unbearable ache, for though watching a Rumblebump laugh is like getting caught in a tidal wave as it breaks, watching a Rumblebump cry (a rare thing indeed) is like standing on the shore while the sea foam swirls around your feet and sucks you deeper and deeper into the soggy sand, until the sea and the sand finally swallow you whole.

The Rumblebumps' words came out in short, painful bursts:

"Smashed."

"Stomped."

"Crushed."

"Broken."

"Ruined."

Sallyroo ran to the stage. "Make it alive," she pleaded, her face as empty as a moonless night. "Make it alive." Behind her, Guafnoggle held out his arms. Cupped gently in his hands was a little orange starfish. Two of its arms were broken off completely, and the end of a third was mashed into a pulp.

"Why? Is it dead?" said Professor Quibble, not very interested.

Guafnoggle answered through his sobs, overwhelmed with grief and completely choked up with punctuation. "Wouldn't, you? Be dead . . . if! you were; torn (in) half?" he said. "Everything is so: fragile."

Trudging behind the Rumblebumps, slowest of all, with his hands covering his downcast face and a crown of seaweed around his head, was Worvil. When he saw Persimmony, he ran to her and threw his arms around her. "Persimmony! Oh, Persimmony, I'm so glad you weren't eaten by a tortoise or carried away by a restless mangrove or lost underground forever! I've had the most awful, wonderful adventure. It was—I mean, when I saw the giant—when I played the flute and lulled him back to sleep—I mean, I—Oh, it's too much to tell. But Persimmony, the starfish is dead and it's all because of me! I put it down on the ground outside the cave, and when the big crowd of people came one of them pushed Guafnoggle and—he didn't know the starfish was there—he fell backward and *stepped* on it with one of his big feet. They'll never let me be Grand Stomper again, and I was just beginning to enjoy it! Please, Persimmony," begged Worvil, his eyes filling with tears. "Help them, Persimmony, please . . ."

Lulled the giant back to sleep? Worvil was a hero after all. "You look taller," Persimmony wanted to say, but couldn't. She placed her hand on top of his head as if to measure him. He looked surprised for a moment, then slowly smiled.

King Lucas had been annoyed at the interruption, but as he gazed down at Guafnoggle's hands he suddenly had an idea. "My dear subjects," he said, pointing to the starfish with new zeal, "that, *that,* THAT is why today I am making a new law." Professor Quibble frowned, since he was usually consulted about all new laws, but Lucas ignored him. "Every single one of us could have been crushed to pieces just like that starfish! Every single one of us could *still* be crushed to pieces like that starfish. So from now on, no one is ever allowed to mention Mount Majestic again. No one may look at it, no one may talk about it, no one may touch it, and above all else no one may ever go up to the top of it. We must always remember that we are a condoomed people—"

"Condemned, Your Highness," whispered Professor Quibble.

"*And* doomed," moaned the steward.

"Both," said Lucas. "Every day, every hour, every minute may be our last. Be thankful for your dinner, hug your family, and cry yourself to sleep every night because you may not see them again the next morning. That is the way life will be from now on. And—"

"But we can't sit here waiting to be destroyed!" someone yelled, and the crowd began to murmur in confusion.

"The giant *might* not wake up for another thousand years."

"And he *might* wake up tomorrow."

"Life will never be the same again."

"Then we must leave the island!"

"Fools!" scoffed the professor. "Where is there to go? How can we escape this fate? We are trapped between a giant and an empty sea!"

"Between a terrible bigness and an everlasting blueness!" said Lucas.

"Between a foot and a wet place!" said the steward.

"But there must be more than the sea," said a small child in the back of the crowd. "Where did the giant come from?"

This was so staggering a question that for several moments there was utter silence. Then from an unnoticed corner of the chaos, Theodore hobbled slowly to the front. His hand gripped his cane and kneaded it softly. He gazed across hundreds of heads to the place where the Smudges stood, and he smiled, and Persimmony felt, as she always felt, that he knew the way out of this trouble.

"Mrs. Amelia Smudge," he said, "I think it's time you told everyone what happened to your husband, Simeon."

Both Persimmony and Prunella turned to their mother in surprise, and Mrs. Smudge began to shrink into her collar and back away into the mass of people behind her.

"I saw it happen, Amelia," the potter prodded. "Seven years ago. I was at the edge of the woods gathering shells by the shore, and I saw a man and a woman down by the water—with a boat."

Mrs. Smudge's eyes bulged, her nose wrinkled, her ears twitched, and her hands flew to cover her mouth as the deep-down smothered secret boiled up inside of her like a sneeze trying to burst out.

"SOAP!" she exploded finally. "The king—King *Lucas*'s father—washed my Simeon's mouth out with soap! And threatened to make us all eat soap until we died if he told anyone about the giant! Of course, Simeon knew no one would believe him even if he *did* tell them what he had seen in the cave. Everyone would have just laughed at him, as they always did whenever he tried to save them. So he built a boat. If the world was big enough to hold a giant, he said, it was big enough for other islands like this one. If he could find an island without a giant on it, everyone could move there and never have to worry about being trampled. He begged and pleaded with me to bring Persimmony and Prunella and come with him. But I wouldn't, because I didn't believe him either . . ." Mrs. Smudge stopped, pulled the handkerchief off her head, and blew her nose in it. "And because I have a moral objection to getting into floating objects of any kind. 'Fools sail off where fishes fear to swim!' I said. 'The proof of the pudding is at the bottom of the sea!' I said. 'There's more than one way to skin a shark!' I said. So he dug a cellar underneath our cottage where the girls and I could hide and be safe if the giant ever woke up, and he shed so many tears that I thought he would sink the boat himself. 'I'll be back,' he promised as he drifted away from me. 'I'll find a home and come back for you.' My husband, my mate, my sweet one, the hero of my heart! I didn't believe him then, but I believe him now. I believe him now!"

The people stood stunned during this extraordinary speech. Theodore said calmly to them, "Yes, if this island is all there is, and we are trapped here with a sleeping giant, we have little hope. But what if Simeon Smudge was right? What if there are things under our feet and things beyond the sea that we have never dreamed of?"

Persimmony gaped at her mother. She looked at her sister, whose mouth was hanging open in astonishment.

Her father had not been eaten by the giant.

The wind heaved a sigh of relief, the waves applauded, the sun did a cartwheel—and so did Persimmony.

Her father had not been eaten by the giant! He had gone to find a home for her.

She looked at the starfish in Guafnoggle's hands. She was the daughter of the Grandest Grand Stomper of All. She wanted to shout. She wanted to sing. The music of the Lyre swelled in her ears again, and she remembered: *Silent hands will speak.*

She stepped away from Worvil and nudged her way through the crowd.

"Persimmony Smudge, don't you dare run away again!" called her mother, but Persimmony kept walking.

Just as she reached the front, however, she slipped on a smashed apple pie and fell into a bed of rotting vegetables. Having nothing else to clean herself with, she took off her beloved blue hat, looked sorrowfully at it just once, and used it to wipe the slop from her dress. Then she shook it out and put it back on her head. Prunella was suddenly standing beside her, quietly clearing away the mess from her sister's path with a broom. Persimmony grinned at her, took the broom, climbed onto the stage, and began to sweep.

Her bare feet squished and slid over melon rinds, mashed bananas, bruised peaches, overturned pumpkin pies, and cracked-open coconuts with the sweet milk spilling out. She swung the broom in big sweeping arcs. As she squished and slid and swung and swept, Persimmony had two thoughts.

The first thought was this: If she had swept the cottage floor as Prunella had told her to, she wouldn't be sweeping up this mess now.

And the second thought was this: If she had swept the floor to begin with, she would never have broken the Giving Pot. And if she hadn't broken the Giving Pot, she would never have lost her hat in the woods. And if she hadn't lost her hat, she would not have heard the Leafeaters' plans. And if she had not heard their plans, no one would have gone to stop them. And if no one had gone to stop them, the giant would have woken up. Yet she was surrounded by people—unstomped, unsmashed, uncrushed, unbroken, unruined—miraculously, wonderfully whole.

Persimmony found this so funny that suddenly there was nothing in the world she wanted to do more than sweep. She leaped and spun and flung out her broom. She smelled the sweet aroma of smashed blueberries oozing between her toes. She felt the sunlight on her face and the sea breeze in her hair, and saw the crisp shape of Mount Majestic against the blue horizon, still standing, still beautiful.

There might be more mountains out there—more islands—more people—more things to do and save and discover and want and be.

Someday she might look out at the sea and see a boat on the horizon, bringing news of a new world. Someday her father might return, and they might have many adventures together.

Worvil was wrong: *Might* was a glorious, glorious word!

"What is she doing?" murmured someone in the crowd.

"She's sweeping."

"No, she's dancing."

"Well, that doesn't seem like a logical thing to be doing at a time like this." Professor Quibble sniffed. A piece of cantaloupe sailed off the end of Persimmony's broom into his mouth, and he fell off the stage choking. Lucas and Chief Rhule soon followed him as bits of food began raining down on their heads.

Just as the Leafeaters had painted color back into their underground world again, Persimmony pretended she was painting the island with the colors of her broom. She painted her mother plum-juice purple and Prunella a bright carroty orange. She painted the Rumblebumps a rich tomato red and the Leafeaters a deep avocado green. She painted the potter a handsome tint of egg yolk and Worvil the pure creamy whiteness of coconut milk. With a bold sweep of her arms, she drew a great glowing arc of pineapple yellow across the Willow Woods and added a splash of peach to the two tortoises.

Had she ever seen before how blue the sky was, how golden the sun? All of it—even the giant—was an unlooked-for, unwelcome, strangely beautiful gift pulled out of a pot.

Tomorrow she would wake up all over again—and what an adventure that would be!

Pushing and swinging the broom along, twirling and spinning in the arms of the wind, weaving a picture with her feet, Persimmony danced before the rising sun and the rising tide and the rising mountain. And as the people watched, they felt their hearts dancing with her.

When the stage was finally clean, Persimmony stood up straight and realized that everyone in the square was *looking* at her. Suddenly she was aware of her ridiculous appearance, and for the first time in her life she wished she were invisible. As gently as if it were made of glass, she laid the broom down at the edge of the stage and went over to where the Rumblebumps stood. Guafnoggle, silently understanding, held the starfish up to her. She took it, wiped away the grime with her apron, took the king's portrait off the bier, and placed the little broken creature there instead.

And there she stood, awkwardly, her task finished. Theodore's eyes were shining with pride. Rheuben Rhinkle's face broke open into a wide smile. He climbed onto the stage, took out a flask from within the folds of his robes, and turned it upside down over the starfish. Persimmony, having tasted that earthy liquid before, knew that it was his tears. When all of the tears were gone, Rheuben sighed deeply, as if a mountain had been lifted off his back.

Chief Rhule nodded, and the rest of the Leafeaters—despite a few muttered comments about "artists"—took out their own flasks and began pouring their tears over the starfish.

King Lucas scowled at the ground in front of him and dug his toe into the dirt. He tried to remind himself how unfair it all was—that this annoying girl's father, this soapy, loopy Simeon Smudge fellow, got to be a hero off sailing somewhere, while his own father was lying next to his mother, buried under a buried castle. But an unfamiliar feeling crept into Lucas and sank its claws painfully deep. Is this what people called a "conscience"? If so, he hated it. A plague upon that cat! It had gotten inside of him. "Wait—stop," he said. He cast one final, longing gaze upon the clay pot, large and stout and fit for a king, the last thing he had in the world. Then he gently lifted Pepper out of it and held the pot up to Chief Rhule. "The starfish needs a coffin."

Rhule set the pot on the bier and put the starfish inside, and the Leafeaters poured their tears into the pot until it was full to the brim. Then slowly, the rest of the islanders stirred from their places and scattered their flower petals over the little coffin. The Rumble-bumps gazed around in swollen-nosed, puffy-eyed wonder. The soft voice of Captain Gidding drifted from somewhere far in the back of the crowd. These were the captain's words:

> *I climbed a hill as high as hope;*
> *I swam a sea as deep as dread;*
> *I bound my fear up with a rope*
> *To hear what Weeping Willow said.*
>
> *I heard her whisper through her sighs:*
> *"The world has lost all dreams but one.*
> *Though night's dark tears may cloud your eyes,*
> *Look—joy is rising with the sun.*

"For fear cannot be bound with rope,
And many swimmers drown in dread;
But no one falls who climbs with hope."
That's what Weeping Willow said.

And so I laid my sorrows by
And sang my beating heart to sleep.
And that, my sighing friend, is why
I'm dancing while the willows weep.

When the captain had stopped, Mrs. Smudge grabbed the broom that Persimmony had left lying on the edge of the stage and began sweeping the ground vigorously right in front of King Lucas. "And that, *that*, THAT," she cried, punctuating each breath with a broomful of banana pulp in the king's face, "is what I think of your new law! No going up on Mount Majestic? No talking about it? What good will all that hushing and fearing and crying do us, I ask you? It won't keep the giant asleep. As long as we're not popping pepper sacks by his nose or sticking shovels in his feet, well, there's nothing better we can do than build a bonfire on top of the mountain and dance for joy. Let sleeping giants lie—that's what I always say."

"Dance for joy on top of the mountain?" said

Lucas. "Don't you see the looks on the faces of my people? The only way they would dance for joy on top of the mountain is if they were looting my castle!"

"Well spoken, Your Highness!" cried Flack. "My fellow citizens, hear the generous words of our king! Generations of kings and queens have filled that castle with the richest treasures to be found anywhere, and he is giving them all to us! All we have to do is go up that mountain and find what's left."

"Wait a minute," sputtered Lucas, "I didn't mean—"

"Just think of the hand-carved furniture, the comfortable mattresses, the silk bedsheets, the silver soupspoons! How many soupspoons would you say were in the castle, Your Highness?"

"What? Oh, about three hundred, but I—"

"Your Highness, this is the greatest thing you have ever done," said Flack, pounding the king on the back. "You will surely be remembered as the most beloved king of all time for this."

"But I didn't . . ." Lucas paused and looked out at the people. "It is? I will?"

"Fellow citizens," continued Flack to the crowd, "who will follow me?"

There was an awkward pause as all eyes turned to

Mount Majestic, green and silent and getting higher by the hour.

"But it's all buried now," said a farmer. "It would take us years to dig through all of that rubble."

The Leafeaters whispered amongst themselves, and Chief Rhule stepped forward. "We," he said impressively, "have *plenty* of shovels."

The islanders hesitated only for a moment. "All I've ever wanted is a comfortable mattress!" one man cried. Others ran after him. As Lucas stood helplessly on the stage, still unsure what had just happened, he saw the same strange, beautiful look glowing in the faces of his subjects that had glowed in Pepper's face the day he had offered his sweet potato soup.

"Hail!" the people shouted gaily. "Hail, King Lucas the Loftier!"

"Aren't you coming?" said Flack, suddenly turning to the king and holding out his hand.

Lucas tried to laugh, but it came out more like a terrified squeak. "Go *up there*? I almost got caught in an exploding castle. I almost died. Why would I want to go back?"

"You have a responsibility to lead your people," said Theodore gently. "Helping them face their fear of the mountain is an awfully good way to begin. You came down, and now it's time to go back up."

"No, please!" cried Lucas, clinging to the edge of the stage as a group advanced toward him. "I don't want to be Lofty anymore! I'll be Lucas the Lowly . . . Lucas the Lenient . . . Lucas the Less Fortunate . . . but please, please, just let me be Lucas the Left Behind!"

Flack and three other pepper mill workers grabbed Lucas's thrashing arms and legs. Mrs. Smudge wrapped her arms around his twisting waist. The steward picked up Pepper the cat. The Leafeaters gathered into marching formation. And together, with the cheers of the people echoing around them, they carried King Lucas back to the top of Mount Majestic.

Persimmony stared after them, laughing. Then she tossed the broom to Prunella, who laughed too. Those who stayed behind with them in the Candlenut town square grabbed brooms and mops and rags and dusters and rakes, and there had never been such a cleaning day recorded in the annals of history. And all the Un-Blue Things that may exist beyond the great blue sea must have seen, that day, a billowing dust cloud rise from an island that may (or may not) be at the Center of Everything. For the giant was not awake yet, and the islanders were kicking their heels and twirling and sweeping and scrubbing with all their might. After all, they said to each other, what more is there to be done? Life is a mess and a miracle. So pick up a broom and dance.

EPILOGUE

I *wish* *I* *could* *tell* you the kingdom was perfectly peaceful and content after that, but if that were so, I would be writing a fairy tale and not a history.

Nubbins the steward, Captain Gidding, and the rest of the soldiers managed, with a great deal of tangled rope and bruised shins, to pitch tents at the top of the mountain where the king and his servants could live until a new castle could be built. This meant that King Lucas had to get used to sleeping on the ground, with twigs and rocks poking through his blankets, and instead of scrumptious suppers prepared in a royal kitchen, he ate much smaller meals cooked over a fire under the stars.

Lucas soon learned that it was a lot more difficult to be the most beloved king of all time than he expected, but he made a valiant effort in the days that followed the falling of the castle. He walked for the first time in his life through the fields and orchards and woods of his kingdom to talk with his subjects face-to-face and share meals at their own humble tables. Of course, it was a bit discumbersomebubblating to walk into a barbershop and see a wig on the broken head of the statue that had once stood in the great hall. And the day he spotted a scarecrow wearing his best robe with the pearl-studded palm trees was a day that tried his soul. But he made sure to compliment the pepper mill workers on their fine new soupspoons, and he made a law that no one was to cut down any trees in the Willow Woods without first getting Chief Rhule's approval.

Of course, King Lionel the Lofty would never have done this. But perhaps (Lucas thought to himself) there is such a thing as being *too* much like one's father. A king must have his own page in the history books, after all. He did not want to end up with a picture of his face on a muddy doormat.

And perhaps (I may add), buried deep within Lucas's own heart, as the Lyre had prophesied, there was still a treasure waiting to be discovered.

People still looked a bit suspiciously at the Leafeaters, and on the Western Shore the Rumblebumps' sadness had mellowed their games and slowed their speech. Despite these odds and ends of discontent, however, the islanders discovered that even though life may never be the same again, it can still be a very good thing indeed. The farmers still whistled in their fields, and the fishermen caught just as many fish as they ever had. The Citizens Against Giants disbanded, and Flack became the new foreman of the pepper mill, which thrived under his just leadership and square meals. In fact, since the king no longer demanded so much pepper, there was plenty of it to go around, and pepper soon became a staple in every household kitchen on the island. Dustin Dexterhoof was put in charge of the excavation of the castle ruins, and the potter returned to his cottage in the Willow Woods, happy once more to make his pots in peace.

The Leafeaters began to invite a few of the more polite villagers down into Willowroot, and when these brave folks returned, their neighbors remarked that there was something different about them—an elegant lift to their heads or a courtesy in their manner—that was rather pleasing. And then there was the matter of the poison-tongued jumping tortoises, who were behaving themselves much better these days.

But towering above all the islanders, with a slowly shrinking mound of ruins on its top and a hidden face slumbering within, was a terrible, majestic Possibility.

As for Persimmony, she swept the floor of her cottage so often and so wildly that Mrs. Smudge and Prunella often had to leave to avoid getting covered with dust (and sometimes furniture). There was an especially joyful day of sweeping, for example, when the Leafeaters' tears finally wore off and Persimmony's voice came back to her. Even more joyful was the day the townspeople of Candlenut erected a statue in the middle of the town square—of a man riding a goat through a sea of apples—with a plaque underneath that said, "To Simeon Smudge: Come back soon and save us." And most joyful of all was the day Rheuben Rhinkle showed up at the Smudges' door with a soggy (but still intact) basket and two (uneaten) pine-needle creations: a turtle and a grasshopper. They smelled strongly of paprika.

A week after what was supposed to be his funeral, King Lucas held his birthday party on top of the mountain, and Persimmony was invited. Mrs. Smudge, after citing all of her moral objections to birthday parties, permitted her daughter to go in the safe company of the potter. It was a joyful celebration full of side-splitting laughter, even though the Rumblebumps were not present. Persimmony, Lucas, Worvil, and the soldiers danced for hours, while Chief Rhule and Rheuben Rhinkle told the other guests wonderful tales of noble rulers and valiant deeds that made them sigh wistfully and vow to be valiant someday too.

At last, it was time to eat. The guests sat on the grass around a large tablecloth lit with candles. The meal was sweet potato soup—without pepper—and pineapple upside-down cake, which King Lucas had thought appropriate considering the present position of the castle. After they had all had their fill, Lucas stood up and cleared his throat.

"I hardly need to say," he said, "that the kingdom is forever indebted to those who followed the call of duty and saved us all from a very flat existence. But there are two people who deserve special honor." He turned to Persimmony, and she felt the color rising to her cheeks. "Persimmony Smudge, talented young basket maker from the cottage at the edge of the woods," he continued, "in appreciation for your extraordinary courage, not to mention your surprising skill with feathers and brooms, I hereby name you the King's Ambidextrous."

Everyone stared at him in silence.

"Um, what exactly are the duties of an 'Ambidextrous,' Your Highness?" Persimmony asked.

"Oh, you know, going on special missions for me, taking important messages to important people, making peace between warring parties, shaking hands . . ."

"Ah! I believe you mean 'Ambassador,'" said Professor Quibble. "'Ambidextrous' means being both right-handed and left-handed."

"Even better. She shall be the King's Ambidextrous Ambassador, and she shall shake hands with twice as many people at once."

This sounded awfully tiring to Persimmony, but it did have a glamorous ring to it. She thanked the king whole-heartedly, even managing a lopsided curtsy. On her head was her blue hat, newly washed, which Jim-Jo Pumpernickel had let her keep after remembering that drowning apple tree hats had just gone out of style. Around her waist was a braided belt of the giant's hair, which Chief Rhule had graciously given back to her once he found out what it was.

Lucas then turned to Worvil. "And to you, Worvil, wherever you come from and whatever you are, I offer a new position in my court (once I have one again). From this day forth you shall be known as the Royal Player of Lullabies. May the music of your flute never fade."

But Worvil blushed deeply and declined, explaining that he had decided to live with the Rumblebumps in his very own cave, which had now been comfortably furnished with a real bed. "I've realized that they *need* me," he said. "After all, they never worry about anything. Somebody's got to teach them about

Mights and Possibilities before it's too late! There's just one thing that bothers me."

"What is it?" Persimmony asked.

"Well, you see," Worvil said, very embarrassed. "For an entire hour this morning, just after I woke up, I wasn't able to worry about anything. I tried and tried, and I simply couldn't. I mean, take the bed for example. If I put it too close to the edge of the cave, a big wave might come while I'm sleeping and flood the cave and sweep me out to sea before I even have time to scream for help. And if I put the bed too far back in the cave, it's so dark there that even when the sun rises I might not wake up. What if no one ever came to wake me and I was asleep underground for a thousand years with no sun, all because of my bed? But this morning, instead of worrying about it, I spent a whole hour listening to the tide coming in instead. What if that happens again? All sorts of terrible things might happen to me because I wasn't ready for them! It's very distressing."

Persimmony sighed and shook her head fondly at her friend. "There you go again, making a mountain out of a molehill."

"Well, there are worse things for a mountain to be made out of!"

"Don't remind me." Persimmony suddenly had

a thought. "You know, you're right: It is best that you live on the Western Shore. Then if the giant ever starts to wake up again, you can run into the cave and play your flute until he falls back to sleep."

"An excellent idea!" said Lucas. "Worvil, you *shall* be the Royal Player of Lullabies."

Worvil was just about to say that he still had plenty of worry left in him, when Theodore rose from where he was sitting. "Now it is time for your last birthday present," the potter said, and he handed Lucas a new clay pot.

Lucas looked at it with surprise and a little bit of suspicion. This pot was simpler than the other one, with no intricate patterns traced on the outside, but it was tall and smooth and noble. He reached his hand inside warily, almost expecting milk again. Instead he felt his hand close around something hard, and when he pulled it out he saw that it was a hammer.

Lucas stared at the hammer in his hands for a moment, then looked back at the stones and splinters that used to be his castle.

"The past is being cleared away," said the potter. "What will you build now?"

The question lingered in the air for a long time. As the guests sat waiting expectantly, they could hear in the distance a low rumbling, growing louder and louder, like a roll of thunder. Worvil groaned, "Of course it *would* storm! I've never known a birthday yet to end well."

But it was not thunder.

Professor Quibble peered hard through the deep blue moonlit darkness to where a new shape was rising in the west. "Impossible!" he said, alarmed. "A tidal wave couldn't reach this high!"

But it was not a tidal wave. At least, not of water.

Around the edge of the castle ruins they came— rolling billows of colorful coats with too many pockets and buttons, tossing crests of long, tangled seaweed-hair, a thunderous roar of big feet pounding the ground as a great host ran and jumped and cart-wheeled toward the little group sitting out under the stars. Just as the king's guests rose from their seats, the wave of Rumblebumps broke upon them.

"It's alive! It's alive! The starfish is alive! It's not dead anymore! We thought it was crushed forever, but tonight we looked in the pot and there it was, all nice and new with its arms back just like it always was. It's alive, it's alive! Have you ever seen anything more wonderful and beautiful and marvelous in the whole wide world? Oh, life is the sunrise, and life is the sea, and life is a game, and life is a pot of tears, and life is a starfish growing its arms back, and now everything is different again . . ." The Rumblebumps hugged everyone they could reach and trampled the tablecloth and knocked over the soup bowls in their excitement. Lucas laughed and Persimmony laughed and the Leafeaters found they could laugh now without a feather to help them. Even Professor Quibble caught himself almost grinning and had to quickly clean his eyeglasses to make sure no one noticed.

But it was soon clear whom the Rumblebumps had really come to find. Guafnoggle opened Worvil's hands and laid the little orange starfish in them, its five arms perfect and whole. A hush fell over the others as they gathered respectfully around him. "You know what to do, Grand Stomper. There's only one thing left to do."

Worvil gazed down at the starfish in his hands, then his face slowly spread into a smile. "To the sea!" he cried. "To the sea!" And he took off running in the direction of the Western Shore. He was followed closely by the Rumblebumps, who were followed by the Leafeaters, who were followed by Lucas, who was followed by Captain Gidding carrying the elderly potter on his back, and the rest kept up as well as they could along the mountain and down the rocky cliffs.

Persimmony paused at the top of the giant's shoulder and looked out toward the invisible horizon between the moon and its glittering, watery reflection. *The world seems so much bigger now that I know you are out there,* she thought.

"Worvil, wait for me!" she called, climbing quickly down the rocks to catch up with the others. And they laughed until they cried, and the tears made their faces shine in the moonlight as they raced to the sea.

All this was related to me in great detail afterward by those present, for I was not invited to the party. No matter. Pineapple upside-down cake makes me dizzy.

So instead I sat at my desk in my new library in the middle of Candlenut, nibbling the nib of a new quill pen, staring out the window at the slow, steady falling of the mountain, and waiting for midnight, when it would begin to rise again.

Breath by breath.

Every breath means another day, and every day is only a breath.

I could have told them, if they'd asked, that—

But never mind. The Lyre-That-Never-Lies has prophesied that, despite all appearances to the contrary, we will live happily ever after. And I believe it.

* THE END *

Glossary
(Who's Who and What's What)

Amelia Smudge: Wife of Simeon Smudge, mother of Persimmony and Prunella, and basket maker with highly sensitive moral feelings and a storehouse of proverbs.

Badly: Substitute herald with a cowd who addoudces visitors by blowing his dose.

Barnabas Quill: Me, your trusty narrator and royal historian.

Barnacle: A revered elderly Rumblebump.

Bathtub: Not a good place for pepper, especially while you are in it.

Captain Gidding: Absentminded but courageous captain of the king's guard, poet, and lover of beauty and butterflies.

Ceremony of Tears: A depressingly doleful Leafeater occasion. Be careful not to drink the tears.

Code of Courtesy: Glossaries should be seen and not heard, so please do not make rude noises or raucous laughter while you are reading this in the middle of the library.

Dustin Dexterhoof: *Dirty* digger, *discoverer* of gold belt buckles, bearer of *bad* news, and, to come to the point, an archaeologist.

FLACK: Leader of the pepper mill rebellion, champion of justice, and defender of turnips and other oppressed things.

FULCRUMB (MR.): The despicable foreman of the pepper mill.

GIANT: Shhhh! Did I say giant?

GIVING POT: What you need is what you get.

GRAND STOMPER: Highly honored title given by the Rumblebumps to anyone who saves a starfish.

GUAFNOGGLE: King Lucas's jester, a Rumblebump full of much laughter and little punctuation.

HAROLD: Herald with a stopped-up trumpet.

JIM-JO PUMPERNICKEL: A peddler with good business sense and a lot of extra colanders to sell.

LEAFEATERS: Reclusive denizens of the secret underground city of Willowroot who love ceremonies, hate rudeness, and (ahem) eat leaves.

LUCAS THE LOFTIER: King of the Island at the Center of Everything, soon to turn thirteen, and craving pepper.

LULU THE LUMINOUS, A.K.A. LULU THE LUDICROUS: Case in point why you should always believe the Lyre-That-Never-Lies.

LYRE-THAT-NEVER-LIES: Prized and unpredictably prophetic musical instrument. Do you believe it?

Mad Sweet Potato Farmer: Case in point why you should always take a deep breath and calm down after hearing traumatic news.

Mount Majestic: It depends on your perspective.

Ned: A pepper mill worker, not very interesting but suffices to move the plot along.

Nubbins: King Lucas's faithful old steward.

Pepper: The blessing and bane of King Lucas's existence, or his cat.

Pepper Mill: A gloomy tower full of drudgery and sneezing.

Persimmony Smudge: If you don't know who she is, I suggest you go back to page 1 and start over.

Poison-Tongued Jumping Tortoise: Spiky, nasty, bouncy, prone to licking, and definitely not a house pet.

Professor Quibble: Geographer, mathematician, philosopher, man of science, advisor to the king, and all-around know-it-all.

Prunella Smudge: Persimmony's very clean but bewildered older sister.

Restless Mangrove: A tree that has not yet found its place in the world.

Rhedgrave Rhinkle: An extremely bitter and uncompromising Leafeater (uncle to Rheuben).

RHEUBEN RHINKLE: An extremely truthful, noble, and artistic Leafeater.

RHIDDLE: An extremely ticklish Leafeater.

RHULE RHODSHOD: Chief of the Leafeaters with a penchant for dandelion hats.

RUMBLEBUMPS: Sea-loving, playful inhabitants of the Western Shore with big hearts, big pockets, and big feet.

SALLYROO: A young Rumblebump girl who wants to catch the moon in her pocket.

SIMEON SMUDGE: Husband of Amelia, father of Prunella and Persimmony, former peppercorn picker, rescuer of anyone who wants to be rescued and many who don't, and mysteriously disappeared hero.

SUNSPITTER: To a Leafeater, anyone who is not a Leafeater.

THEODORE THE WISE: Elderly potter who makes Giving Pots, careful studier of the Lyre's prophecies, protector of young girls lost in the woods, and in general someone you should probably listen to.

TODDLE: An overburdened donkey.

TURNIP: A controversial vegetable.

WORVIL: A worrier, but we love him anyway.